Lea and Camila

by Lisa Yee
and Kellen Hertz

★ American Girl

Contents

To Mary See
Thank you for always being there for me.

— L. Y.

For my grandmother Terry,
who never let her fears stop her.
Thank you for showing me what it
means to live life to the fullest.

— K. H.

Camila Is Coming!
Chapter 1

"**L**ea, how's the cake coming?" my mom asked as she looked over at me from the island in the center of our sunny kitchen.

"Good!" I replied. I was perched in our corner breakfast nook, surrounded by eggs, sugar, butter, cream cheese, flour, and our bright red mixer, which Mom had set up just for me. I cracked two eggs into the bowl of the mixer and studied my recipe.

"I think that's everything . . . Oh wait, vanilla!" I jumped off my chair and did a running slide in my socks over to the spice cabinet.

"Slow down, honey," Mom laughed. "It's not a race!"

I nodded, standing on tiptoe to grab the vanilla. I knew she was right—but I was so giddy, it was impossible to slow down. In just a few hours, the girl

I'd met two months ago in Brazil, Camila Cavalcante, was arriving in St. Louis to stay with us for an *entire week*! My stomach did an excited flip. Yesterday in class, I'd been counting the minutes until spring break arrived, but ever since I'd woken up this morning, time felt like it was flying ... and so was I.

I measured out the vanilla and poured it over the other ingredients. In honor of Camila's arrival, I was making my favorite dessert—gooey butter cake, a St. Louis tradition. I'd made it before with my mom's help, but this was the first time I was baking on my own. I turned on the mixer. As I listened to the soothing sound and watched the paddle whip everything into a rich golden batter, I took what felt like my first real breath of the day.

I'd already straightened up my older brother Zac's room, where Camila would be sleeping. Plus I'd cleaned my room, and now it was so neat that I didn't even recognize it! I'd also changed the water in my pet turtle Ginger's aquarium, although she didn't exactly seem grateful. But then, Ginger wasn't big on expressions. Turtles seldom are.

Before starting the gooey butter cake, I'd made

sure to set the dining room table for the welcome dinner we were having for Camila. The fancy place settings made it feel as if we were having Christmas in April.

Mom came over and peered at the buttery yellow batter as I turned off the mixer. "Looks pretty gooey," she said, smiling. She stuck in a pinkie and tasted the batter. "Perfect-o!" she exclaimed. Without missing a beat, she handed me the baking dish we always used for gooey butter cake.

She watched as I carefully poured the batter into the pan. It was hard to keep steady when all I could think of was the creamy, sweet gooey butter cake still warm from the oven!

As the cake began to bake, I set the timer.

"There," my mother sighed. "Task #14 done."

"Only 437 more to go!" I said cheerfully.

Mom laughed, but she looked tired. With a full-time job plus taking care of our family, she was always busy, and today was no exception. Mom was making toasted ravioli, Caesar salad, and her famous garlic bread, all from scratch, to welcome Camila.

"Did you clear out a few drawers in Zac's room

for Camila to use?" Mom asked.

"Oh no, I forgot!" I said. "I'll go do it now."
I think my mother could sense that I was mad at
myself, because as I crossed to the doorway, she
called after me.

"Sweetheart?" she said gently. "It's okay if
everything isn't exactly perfect. I'm sure Camila will
just be happy to see you." I knew she was right, but I
couldn't help thinking, *Camila's never been to St. Louis
before. I want to make sure she loves it.*

I ran down the hall to the front entry and hustled
up the stairs, holding the banister. Our house is more
than a hundred years old, and Dad always jokes that
it's held together by charm. It's kind of true—the
stairs lean a little, and none of the doors stay shut.
Still, I love it. My mom says it's "a typical Second
Empire Victorian," but its high tin ceilings and
curlicue woodwork make me feel like we live in
a life-size dollhouse.

I stopped to catch my breath on the landing,
plopping onto the worn purple velvet bench seat

by the bay window. I love the view from here onto Hickory Street, where we live. Below, old maple trees line the block, shading the brick row houses painted in bright hues of blue and pink and yellow. Our neighborhood is known as Lafayette Square. At its heart is Lafayette Park, an elegant garden with wrought-iron gates and a gurgling fountain. Although the houses are old, the lively shops and restaurants make it feel like a quirky mix of old and new, past and present—just how my parents like it.

"Lafayette Square suits our family," Dad often says, and I have to agree. Both of my parents like looking at old things in new ways. My father teaches history at Washington University, and my mother is an architect specializing in restoring old buildings. They renovated our house together when my brother Zac was little. Every time I walk through the rooms, I feel like the house is a treasure my parents found and saved for me.

In Zac's room, as I cleared his old clothes out of two dresser drawers for Camila to use, I screamed when I came across his rubber snake collection. Zac! Even though he was far away, he could still make

me laugh. His walls were plastered with posters of
the Grand Canyon and icy Antarctica next to action
shots of pro surfers. Like my grandmother Ama,
my brother loves to travel and explore the outdoors.
That's a big reason why he'd decided to study
abroad for his last year of college. Back in February,
I'd gone with my parents to visit Zac in Brazil. It
was the most incredible trip ever. Although it was
far from easy (we got lost in the jungle, and my
dad broke his leg), I got over my fear of the ocean,
rescued a baby sloth . . . and met Camila!

Zac was still in Brazil, doing research on poaching in the Amazon rainforest. I tried to picture what
he might be doing right now—taking photographs
of a rare insect, or canoeing past a caiman. For a
moment, I wished I could be there with him. Then
I thought, *No . . . Camila and I are going to have our own
adventure here!*

Camila and I had gotten along so well in Praia
Tropical, the Brazilian seaside town where we met.
She was always laughing, always moving, and was
full of questions about my life in St. Louis. We'd been
sending each other jokes and photos over e-mail ever

since we met. When Camila mentioned she was
going with her parents to visit relatives in Chicago,
I'd suggested that she come to St. Louis afterward.
It's only a half-hour flight, but I don't think either
of us really expected our parents would agree to it.
When they did, my heart did a happy cartwheel.

"I think it'll be a great experience for both of
you girls," my mom had said, "especially since
you've been able to keep your friendship going
from so far away." Camila had already flown with
her family all the way from Brazil. Now she was
flying here from Chicago all on her own. She was
definitely adventurous.

As I walked out of Zac's room, Dad called to me
from downstairs. "Lea!" he said. "We need to head to
the airport in five."

The airport! Camila! "Okay!" I said, and ducked
into my room. I grabbed my sweater and took a
look around. Ginger was napping on her favorite
rock in her tank, worn out from the morning's
activity. My bed was made, its floral quilt folded
neatly below the scrolled wood headboard, and my
journal lay facedown on my desk where I'd been

writing in it that morning. Of course, it wasn't just my journal. Originally the red leather-bound book had been Ama's diary, one of many she kept over the years as she traveled the world. After she died, I'd taken her journals with me on our trip to Brazil. They inspired me so much that I'd decided to pick up where Ama had left off—recording my own travel adventures.

I turned over the journal and looked at my most recent entry.

Dear Journal,

Although I'm only traveling to the airport and back today, it still counts as an adventure, because CAMILA IS ARRIVING AND I AM SO EXCITED! Can you tell? :) I can't wait to see her again, and show her all the great things about St. Louis!

When I came downstairs, it smelled like a bakery. Dad was waiting for me. I looked through the oven's glass window. Golden bubbles were forming on top of the gooey butter cake. I inhaled

the delicious scent. "Behave while I'm gone,"
I ordered the cake.

"Don't worry," laughed Mom. "Your cake will
be here when you get back. And so will Camila!"

✪

"What are you going to show Camila while she's
here?" my father asked me as we entered the freeway
ramp.

I began to list everything I'd been thinking. "The
Arch, Grant's Farm, City Museum, the Mississippi
steamboats, the Opera House . . ."

"Hold on," said Dad, changing lanes toward the
airport. "That might be too ambitious. Camila's only
here for eight days. Don't forget, you two are doing
that photography class at COCA."

Yes! How could I forget? COCA is the Center of
Creative Arts, one of the coolest places in St. Louis.
Every school vacation they hold a day camp for kids.
In the summer it's usually for the performing arts,
but during spring break they were holding a visual
arts camp, and Camila and I were enrolled in the
photography class. I'd convinced my best friend

Abby to take the class with us, too. I just hoped she and Camila would get along.

Taking photos is one of my favorite things to do. My blog about the Amazon rainforest is filled with photos I took when I was there. On the weekends, Abby and I like to walk her dog around our neighborhood, and all around are interesting things for me to photograph. Once I took a photo of a man walking down the street with his pet ferret on his shoulder, and in the picture, he and the ferret had the exact same look on their faces! I love watching the world go by until I see a picture I want to take. When that happens, it feels like everything slows down and comes into focus.

Dad had arranged for us to meet Camila at the flight arrival gate. We waited as passengers streamed through the open doors. Finally, Camila appeared. She looked a little lost, but as soon as she saw me, she burst into a smile. I ran up and with a little hop, she hugged me.

"How was your flight?" I asked as we headed to the baggage area. "Okay," she replied. "I am glad it was short." I nodded, remembering that Camila was afraid of heights. "I closed the window shade to try to forget we were in the clouds," she said, frowning.

Camila's bright purple bag was waiting at the luggage carousel. Dad picked it up, and we started back to the car. A breeze hit us when we exited the terminal, and Camila shivered. "I did not think it would be so cold right now," she said. "Usually, we visit in summer."

"It's actually pretty warm for April," I replied, but Camila wrapped her arms around herself as if she was freezing.

As Dad drove home, Camila looked out at the gray skyline. I couldn't tell what she was feeling, so I just kept talking. I talked about Lafayette Square, and camp, and photography, and Abby, who couldn't wait to meet her.

"My best friend Abby's mother is a veterinarian, and their house is like a rescue shelter," I told her. "They have a dog and two cats and a parrot and a new puppy named Tiny that they're fostering. We can go over and play with them, since she just lives two blocks away."

Camila gave a faint smile, pressing her cheek

against the window, and closed her eyes.

Was it my imagination, or did Camila seem less than excited to be here? *She's probably just tired*, I said to myself, but worry started digging into my stomach. *What if Camila thinks St. Louis is boring?* Brazil is colorful and dramatic, with its huge rainforest full of wild monkeys and sloths, and its endless beaches. Everything is warm there, even the ocean. Compared to that, St. Louis could seem kind of blah.

I looked out the window. The passing stone buildings and trees blended together in a dull grayness. I sighed. Then, in the distance, something caught my eye. It was the gleaming silver loop of the Gateway Arch. Seeing it somehow made me feel better. *St. Louis is great*, I reminded myself. *I just have to make sure Camila has an amazing time, that's all.*

Seeing in a New Way
Chapter 2

Camila's welcome dinner flew by in a whirl of food and laughter. My father made sure to keep the bad puns coming. "Don't mind my *cheesy* sense of humor," he said to Camila as he handed her the basket of mozzarella garlic bread.

"Ugh, *Dad*!" I said, shaking my head, but Camila laughed. Although she hadn't said much, she seemed happier than she had been in the car, especially when I started talking about all the places I wanted to show her.

"You have to see the Arch close up, obviously," I said. "Hopefully we'll also have time to go to Grant's Farm. They have *dozens* of horses and a huge petting zoo," I told her. "Oh, and we have to go see my mom's new project! She's helping to rebuild an old mansion."

Camila looked interested. "Really?" she said to my mom. "This is what you do?" My mother nodded.

"She takes old buildings that are about to collapse and fixes them so they're as good as new, or better," I explained. I'd seen photographs of some of the houses my mom had restored, but I'd never been to one of her building sites before. I loved the idea of visiting.

As Dad served gooey butter cake, I told Camila it was a St. Louis specialty. I watched as she took her first bite.

Her eyes lit up and she smiled. "It is sweet!"

"Lea made it for you," my mom told her.

"It's my favorite dessert," I added.

Camila nodded, her mouth full. "I think now it is *my* favorite, too!"

After dinner, when we finished clearing the dishes, I took Camila upstairs to show her my room.

On the stairs, she paused. "Is this your grand-mother?" she asked, looking at the photographs lining the staircase wall. She pointed to a picture of Ama in a snorkeling mask in Bali.

"That's her," I said. In the photo, Ama was beaming and giving a thumbs-up. Around her neck

Seeing in a New Way

hung the compass necklace she always wore.

I squinted again at Ama's picture. I could just barely make out the flower on the compass's face. I'd never seen another compass like it before. Looking at it, I felt sadness wash over me. I had left Ama's necklace in Brazil, as an offering to the Goddess of the Sea, Yemanjá. I knew I had done the right thing, but part of me wished the compass was still hanging around my neck, to remind me of my grandmother.

I showed Camila the other pictures of Ama on the wall. There were photographs of her at all different ages—with Grandpa Bill on their wedding day in 1960, and then later, with my mom as a baby. Mostly, though, there were photos of her exploring: surfing in Mexico, cross-country skiing in Siberia, and skydiving with Zac on his eighteenth birthday. I loved the shot of her leaping over a boulder on Bondi Beach in Australia, hair flying. The look of sheer joy on her face seemed to lift her up. Although Ama hadn't started traveling until she retired, she was still the most adventurous person I'd met. *"I'm not fearless,"* she used to say, *"but I don't let my fear stop me."* When I looked at all the photos of her,

pride swirled with sadness inside me.

"Your grandmother was a very unusual person," Camila said.

I nodded. Worried that I might cry, I swallowed hard and changed the subject. "Do you want to see my room?"

The minute Camila started looking around my bedroom, I felt a little nervous. My walls were covered in a jumble of maps and photos. I wished I had put away the *National Geographic* magazines stacked on my night table and piled by my bed. Camila didn't seem to notice all my things, though. The second she spotted my turtle, she headed over to her tank.

"Ginger is so cute!" Camila exclaimed. "Even cuter than in pictures." Ginger lifted her head up to look at Camila. I showed Camila how Ginger liked it when I scratched her under her scaly chin, and how to pick her up. Camila stood, cradling Ginger and squinting at a map of India with a dozen tiny colored pins stuck in it. "Why have you put these here?" she asked.

"Those are all the cities in India I want to visit,"

Seeing in a New Way

I told her. "Delhi, Mumbai, Jaipur, Agra . . . Every
time I see a photo of a place I want to go, I put it
on the wall with a map." Camila wandered around,
looking at the maps of Japan, Paris, Tangier, and the
Galápagos Islands. "I once made a list of all the
places I wanted to go," I explained, "but I kept
adding to it so I ran out of space. It was just easier to
put up maps and photos instead."

"Where is the map of St. Louis?" Camila asked.

"I don't have one," I said.

Camila raised her eyebrows, surprised. "Why
not?" she replied.

"Because it's my hometown," I said, shrugging.
"I already know all about St. Louis."

My eyes came to rest on the most recent photo
I'd added to the wall. It was a shot of me with Camila
on the beach. We were wearing swimsuits and
colorful wish bracelets. Looking at the picture made
me happy—and a bit nervous. Brazil was like a
festive party dress. Compared to it, St. Louis seemed
like jeans and sneakers.

After Camila turned in for the night, I checked my tablet. I had a new e-mail from Zac! Ever since he went to Brazil, it had been tough to keep in touch, especially lately. Last week he had moved from the town of Santa Sofia, where he'd been living with the Barros family, to Manaus, a large city in the middle of the Amazon rainforest. He was now doing research and working at an animal sanctuary. I hadn't heard from him since the move, so I was excited to get an e-mail.

Hey, Lea,

Hope you're enjoying your reunion with Camila. Things are good here. The Manaus sanctuary is smaller than the one near Santa Sofia that took care of Amanda, but they really need me here, so I'm getting to do a lot for the animals. Yesterday I helped rescue a pair of baby macaw parrots! I'll try to send some pictures soon. Give Mom, Dad, and Camila big hugs for me.
xoxo Z

🌿 Seeing in a New Way 🌿

Warmth wrapped around me. I loved knowing that Zac was helping animals. He and I had worked together to rescue Amanda, an orphaned baby sloth. We had found her alone in the forest, weak and injured, and taken her to a wildlife sanctuary near Santa Sofia. I had helped them treat her and nurse her back to health. Amanda was still growing and getting stronger, and the vet there, Erika, sent me adorable pictures of her every week. Sloths are so cute! I couldn't wait to see Zac's pictures of the animals he was working with.

⭐

The next morning, Dad dropped us off at the Center of Creative Arts for the first day of photography camp. COCA is a sleek glass and metal building. Although it looks very modern, it's already a local landmark. A few years earlier, they'd done a big renovation to restore it to look exactly as it did when it was built. Mom had worked on the project, so whenever I went there, I felt especially proud.

Kids were swarming the registration desks by the front entrance. Once we checked in, we pushed

through a pair of huge glass doors into the busy
lobby. Along the back wall stretched a tile mosaic of
the St. Louis skyline against a swirling starry sky.
Camila looked around, excited. "Wow," she said.
"Can we take a selfie?"

"Yes!" I exclaimed. We crammed together in
front of the mosaic. I lifted up my camera, but as
I snapped, someone jostled me from behind.

"Lea!" It was my best friend Abby, wearing a
grin as wide as her headband. Her thick black curly
hair was pulled up in two mini buns, and she was
wearing a plaid dress, red tights, and her usual
round-framed glasses. Abby's mom is black and her
dad is white, and with her mom's broad smile and
her dad's loud laugh, she's a perfect blend of them.
Like me, she loves animals. Having so many rescue
pets means Abby's always covered in pet hair, but
she doesn't mind. She says what she means and
doesn't care what anyone thinks of her—two reasons
why I really like her.

Before I could say, "You photobombed our
selfie!" Abby started shaking Camila's hand, laughing and peppering her with questions.

Seeing in a New Way

"Camila, right?! You look just like your photo. I'm Abby Hudson. So, what do you think of St. Louis? Have you been here before?"

I could tell that Camila didn't understand everything, but she tried to keep up with Abby's questions. "Nice to meet you, Abby . . . No, I have never before been to St. Louis . . ."

As we walked to class, Abby paused for a second. "Honestly, you guys, I'm worried about taking photography. What if I'm bad at it?" She grimaced. "I usually spend spring break playing soccer at the community center."

"I love soccer!" Camila said enthusiastically. "I play forward."

"Cool!" Abby said. "I'm a goalie. I also play the oboe. I like taking photos with my phone, but I'm not like Lea here—she's an *expert*." She grinned at me.

"I'm not," I said, modest.

"Well, you're more of an expert than me," Abby insisted. "You took third place in a national photography contest last year."

"I am also not an expert," Camila confessed, sounding relieved that she wasn't the only one.

21

"Great!" Abby told her. "We can be beginners together!"

When we walked into class, six kids were already there, sitting in front of sleek silver computers. The walls were lined with posters of different photographs. A tiny short-haired woman wearing big jingly earrings stood up front. She waved to us as we came in.

"Our last photographers have arrived!" she said. "Welcome! I'm Nedra Garcia, a.k.a. Ms. Garcia, and I'll be your teacher. Please, pick a computer."

Camila sat between Abby and me in the front row. Ms. Garcia gave us a friendly smile as she handed out digital cameras to the students who hadn't brought one.

"Make sure you take good care of these," she said. "Now, before I talk about what we're going to do, I want to hear what each of you hopes to get out of this class. So speak up."

Kids started raising their hands. Most of them wanted to learn Photoshop to get rid of mistakes or shadows in their photos. A red-haired boy named Kevin wanted to learn how to use Instagram better.

Seeing in a New Way

Abby waved her hand. "I want to learn how to take a photo without accidentally putting my thumb in front of the lens," she said. A few kids laughed. "It's true! It happens a *lot!*"

"I think you'll find it easier to avoid that with a real camera, if you're used to using a phone," said Ms. Garcia with a smile. Her eyes flicked over to me. "And what about you—"

"Lea," I said. "I just want to learn how to take better photographs."

"That's a great goal," Ms. Garcia replied. Her earrings swayed as she nodded. She looked around the room at the class. "This week, I'll be teaching the basics of Photoshop. You'll learn how to set filters, crop, and adjust color and brightness, all basic skills in digital photography. I should warn you, however, that knowing how to erase red-eye is not the same thing as learning how to take a good photograph."

Ms. Garcia turned to look straight at me. "That's because a good photo isn't about filters or lenses or photo apps. It's about how you look at the world. A good photographer is always trying to see things in a new way, to discover what's being overlooked, to

show the viewers something they've never seen before, or show it in a *way* they've never seen before."

Confusion clouded my thoughts. I knew I was good at photography. Everyone said my photos were great. But I didn't really know what Ms. Garcia meant by "seeing in a new way."

Ms. Garcia walked over to a poster of a vintage-looking black-and-white photo. In it, a woman in a black evening dress stood between two elephants, her arms elegantly stretching to touch their curving trunks.

"This photograph is a classic," said Ms. Garcia. "It was taken by Richard Avedon. There are many reasons why it's so good, but the main reason is . . . have you *ever* seen a woman in a dress like this with two elephants?"

I hadn't.

"It's totally unexpected," she explained, "which makes it memorable. Not only that, but the lighting, the positioning, the focus and composition all work together to make it unique and beautiful."

Ms. Garcia moved to another black-and-white photo, of a group of workmen eating lunch sitting on a steel beam ... thousands of feet in the air above a city!

"No one knows who took this picture," she said. "At first glance it looks perfectly normal, right? Just a group of men having lunch at work suspended in midair. Yet it's also extraordinary, because it gives you a perspective on the city, and on construction workers, that the public had never seen before it was published."

Finally, Ms. Garcia crossed to a color photo of a young girl. She was wearing a red headscarf, and her sea-green eyes stared straight into the camera. Excitement bubbled inside me as I recognized her. *I know that picture!* I thought. *It's from **National Geographic**!*

"This image isn't of something unusual," Ms. Garcia continued. "It's a simple portrait of a girl from Afghanistan. What makes it distinctive is how the photographer captures her intense expression. Looking at her face, you see the world through her eyes for a moment."

I silently agreed. *I wonder if I'll be able to take a picture that good someday*, I mused.

Lea and Camila

"So now, it's your turn," Ms. Garcia said. Again, it seemed like she was talking right to me, until I realized she was looking at the whole class. "I want each of you to go out there and take a photograph of something that you think is unusual or memorable. You have ten minutes to go anywhere on this floor, starting ... *now!*"

We all looked at one another. Ms. Garcia waved us along, grinning. "Go on. Time's running out!"

I jumped up. I knew exactly what I wanted to photograph.

I headed straight to the mosaic of St. Louis at night, in the lobby. Up close, the starry sky was made up of tiny tiles in a hundred different shades of blue dappled with silver. They fit together like shimmering puzzle pieces. I had an urge to take a close-up of a patch of tiles, but then I got worried—what if no one could tell what I had photographed? I didn't want that. So I stepped backward. Keeping the mosaic perfectly centered in my frame, I took several shots, then looked at the photos in the viewer. They were all in focus, but the second shot was my favorite. I deleted all the other ones.

Seeing in a New Way

When everyone got back to class, Ms. Garcia downloaded our photographs onto her computer. We gathered around and looked at the pictures one by one.

"Don't say which one you took," she told us. "Let's just talk about what we think of each."

There were pictures of the sky, and the lobby, and the main COCA sign. One boy had taken a photograph of himself in a mirror. It was blurry but still nice. "I like the angle," said Ms. Garcia.

Finally, my photograph of the mosaic popped up. Ms. Garcia looked at it for a long moment, considering. "This photograph is very nicely composed."

"What does that mean?" someone asked.

"It means the photographer is thinking about the position of the camera to the subject, and where objects are in the frame," Ms. Garcia said. I blushed, pleased. "If I had to identify one aspect of it to be improved," she continued, "it's that it could be more . . . surprising."

I felt myself turn red again—and this time, it wasn't with pride. What did she mean, *surprising*?

"Still, it's a very pretty picture," said Ms. Garcia,

but I barely heard her. My cheeks were on fire
as we made our way back to our seats. What did
Ms. Garcia mean? Was she saying that my picture
was ... *boring*?!

Ms. Garcia's voice broke into my thoughts.
"Don't worry," she said. "You're all going to have
plenty of chances this week to take photos and
improve your skills. Every morning, we will become
'urban explorers.' We'll be visiting different neighborhoods to take photographs. Some areas you may
know and some you may not, but hopefully you'll all
discover and photograph parts of St. Louis that you
didn't know existed. After all, this city's been around
for two hundred and fifty years. There's a lot more
here than frozen custard and Cardinals baseball
games," she said, grinning. "Not that those things
aren't great."

"They *are*," Abby whispered to Camila, who
giggled.

"Your goal will be to learn to see things in a new
way," said Ms. Garcia. "On the last day of camp,
you'll select and frame your best work, and it will be
part of a camp-wide evening art show so your family

and friends can see what you've created. Some of the images will also be selected for publishing in the fall issue of COCA's magazine."

Abby nudged me. "I bet they'll pick one of your pictures, Lea," she said. "You're a *great* photographer!"

My stomach sank. It was nice that Abby had confidence in me, but after everything Ms. Garcia had said, I knew that if I was going to take a photograph that was really great, I had a *lot* of work to do.

Coventry House

Chapter 3

After camp, my dad picked Camila and me up in the station wagon. Normally he would be busy teaching history and grading papers, but since he was on sabbatical this semester, this week he was our driver.

"How was photography class?" Dad asked.

"All right," I said, thinking back to Ms. Garcia's comment that good photographers push themselves to "see in a new way." I had no idea what she meant, so how was I ever going to become a better photographer?

"It was very good, Mr. Clark," Camila volunteered from the backseat. "I think I'll learn a lot. And Lea and I will both take some good pictures for the art show."

My dad perked up. "There's a show, huh?"

Camila told Dad all about the final exhibition at the end of camp.

He looked impressed. "Sounds exciting. I can't wait to see what *develops*!"

My father had a doctor's appointment to see how his broken leg was healing, so he was dropping us off with Mom at her work site. As we turned onto the street where her building was, I noticed that the houses here were much bigger than the ones on Hickory Street. Some had boarded-up windows. A few even looked like they were about to fall down.

"This is Old North St. Louis," Dad said as he turned a corner. "It's one of the city's most historic neighborhoods. Many of these houses were built around the same time as ours was." Our car rolled to a stop. "Here we are!"

Before us stretched a dark stone building as wide as three regular houses put together. It had huge curved front windows and a front door that seemed tall enough for a giraffe to walk through, with polished green stone columns on either side. As I looked up, I saw why the house needed my mother. The upper levels were sagging, and parts

seemed to be missing. Plywood covered most of the windows on the third floor, and the slate roof had large bald patches. Crumbling turrets crowned each of the house's corners. It reminded me of a ruined castle.

"It's so beautiful," Camila said reverently as we walked up the front steps. I agreed.

A rusty knocker hung on the front door, but Dad just reached forward and turned the doorknob. Camila and I followed him through a wood-paneled entry hall, past a dark double staircase sailing up beneath a dusty chandelier.

Dad waved us through a side archway into one of the biggest rooms I'd ever seen. It was easily the size of my school cafeteria, with carved stone fireplaces at either end big enough for me and Camila to stand in. The fireplace close to us had been restored to a clean, blue-gray marble, but the far one was still blackened with dirt and soot. In between, the room was buzzing with activity. Workers moved around different tables, sawing, sanding, and nailing. When I spotted my mom at a wide table looking over some blueprints with a man in a hard hat, I felt a burst of

pride. I'd always imagined she had a cool job, but actually *seeing* what she was doing suddenly made everything so real.

Mom smiled when she saw us. "Welcome to Coventry House," she said as she headed toward us.

Once Dad left for his appointment, my mother gave me and Camila the grand tour. "The mansion was built in 1894 by a candy-maker named Francis Coventry, for his wife and three daughters," she began. "This hall is known as the Great Room. For the moment, it's our main work area." She led us through the space, weaving around two men moving lumber and a woman chipping rust off an old metal window frame, until we reached an archway that opened onto a long hallway. We followed her down the hall past different rooms. As we came to each one, Mom pointed out details I hadn't noticed, such as a cluster of carved violins crowning the doorway to the music room, and baskets of fruit and a roast goose over the mantel in the dining room. "Coventry wanted his home to be special, so he employed master carvers to decorate each room in a unique way," she said.

 Lea and Camila

The more I looked, the more there was to see. It felt sort of like when I was on the Amazon River, realizing how much there was to see all around me. I thought of what Ms. Garcia had said about looking at things in new ways.

We were about to leave the dining room when Camila stopped at a door. She peered at a brass knob stamped with a curving design that looked familiar. "What is this?" Camila asked Mom, pointing to it.

"That is a *fleur-de-lis*, the symbol of St. Louis," my mom replied. "It was originally a symbol for the King of France, who once owned this whole area."

"It's a flower, right?" I said, remembering what she had once told me.

Mom nodded. "Yes—'*fleur*' means flower. It's a stylized drawing of a lily or iris. Mr. Coventry wanted them in all the rooms, to remind him of how much wealth the city had given him. Of course, they also represent royalty," she said, winking, "so he also might have wanted to feel like a king."

We walked out of the dining room, past a sunlit porch. "After the last of Coventry's daughters died, the house was sold," Mom continued. "It was turned

into an orphanage, then a girls' school, and finally a boardinghouse, before it was abandoned. Since then, it's been vandalized, flooded, and part of it even burned down in a fire. No one wanted it, and the city was thinking about tearing it down."

"I can't believe that!" I said, indignant.

"There are a lot of great old buildings that no one wants anymore," said Mom. "Luckily, people are trying to save them. A few years ago, the Old North St. Louis Preservation Society started raising money to fix Coventry House. They've rebuilt many homes in this area, which is great for the neighborhood. The preservation society has teamed up with a private donor to raise enough money to restore Coventry House, so it can become a community center. When the center opens, it will serve the residents already here, and hopefully also make more people want to move to the neighborhood and bring even more houses back to life."

"Mom," I said proudly, "*you* are bringing Coventry House back to life!"

"Not just me," she said, smiling. "A lot of people are working to save this place. Although I do feel

Lea and Camila

I have a personal connection to the house through Ama. This was one of her favorite buildings in St. Louis."

"Really?" I asked.

Mom nodded. "Ama lived in this neighborhood until she was 14, before they moved to West County."

I'd never known Ama had lived nearby. It made me wonder what else I didn't know about her.

As we peeked into another room, I couldn't help picturing my grandmother here, her compass necklace gleaming around her neck. Ama loved exploring—she would have wanted to explore every nook of this strange, beautiful house.

We passed through an archway and Mom stopped. "Here we are!"

I realized we'd gone all the way around and returned to the front entry hall. The double staircase curved gracefully behind us, but I could see now that rusty metal gates were locked at the top of each set of steps.

"Can we go upstairs?" I asked.

"The second and third floors are still off-limits except to the construction crew," she said. "But come

on, I'll show you one more thing."

Mom turned around and moved to a corner of the wood-paneled foyer wall. When she pressed it in, it sprang back, opening like a door!

"Whoa," I exclaimed as my mother led us into a semicircular room with curved windows. "Coventry's daughters asked their father for a special room away from servants and guests, where they could relax and read," she told us. "So he built them this morning room."

I looked around. Opposite us, a young woman in painter's overalls stood on a ladder by a strip of wall.

"Camila and Lea, this is Sarah," Mom said. Sarah pulled her earbuds out and grinned at us. "Sarah studies art restoration at Wash U. She volunteered to help uncover one of Coventry House's hidden treasures—this mural." I looked at the wall. Most of the top plaster had been chipped away. Under the cloudy layers that remained, I could see faint, shadowy outlines.

"What is a mural?" asked Camila.

"A wall painting," answered Mom. "Coventry

wrote that he was going to have a mural painted for his daughters. It's noted in the blueprints. Unfortunately, we have no photographs of it, so we won't know exactly what it is until Sarah's finished."

Just then, the door behind us opened. The man in the hard hat popped his head in.

"There you are," he said to Mom. "The bank's on the phone," he told her. "The donor's payment is late."

My mother sighed. "Again?" she said, sounding upset, and then she stopped herself. She turned to us. "I'm sorry, girls. I need to go take this call."

"Can we stay and watch Sarah work on the mural?" I asked.

Mom nodded. "Just don't wander off. Come back to the Great Room when you're done watching."

After Mom left, we watched Sarah work. She'd pry off bits of plaster with a tiny knife, then use a fan-shaped brush to skim away dust. After a moment, I thought I could see the outline of a girl's face emerging, with wide eyes and a bow-shaped mouth.

As I strained to look at it, a faint, high-pitched sound came from nearby. *A ghost?* Big old houses are

often haunted. I glanced at Camila. From her face, I could tell she'd heard it too. The sound came again, more insistent. It seemed to be coming from behind a nearby door. Camila moved to open the door, but I stopped her.

"Wait." I bent down, putting my eye to the old-fashioned keyhole. All I could see was a drab, dusty back hallway—until a small cat with black fur and white paws whisked across it! I gasped. The cat paused. With its skinny legs and giant eyes, it was more of an older kitten than a grown-up cat.

"It's a kitten," I whispered to Camila, but before I could say maybe we should try not to scare it, Camila pushed open the door. In a flash, the kitten bolted down the hall, zipping around a corner.

"Come on!" Camila said, bouncing with excitement.

I glanced back. Sarah had her earbuds in and was facing away from us, but I still felt nervous. "Hold on," I cautioned, but Camila was already a few steps down the hall. "Mom said not to go too far." Still, I was as excited as Camila. I love animals, and what if this kitten needed our help?

In the distance, I heard the tiny mew again. We crept down the dark hall, trying to be quiet. The wood floor was dirty and uneven, and the boards creaked with each step. The walls had rough, splintery holes where plaster had fallen off. Somewhere in front of us, I could hear tiny claws skittering. *The kitten!*

We kept moving. Ahead on the right was a door, slightly ajar. Using one finger, I swung the door open to reveal a pile of old wood planks in a roomy closet. Rusty nails stuck out from some of the boards. Camila leaned over the pile. My excitement turned to fear and I grabbed her arm. "Careful!"

Camila nodded. We eased around the wood, looking for the kitten. Through some gaps in the pile, we spotted the kitten hiding inside. It was black except for its white nose and feet and a pair of golden, terrified eyes. Seeing us, it froze in place and let out the tiniest, cutest hiss in the world.

"*Shhh . . .*" I told the kitten, trying to calm it, as Camila slowly crouched. But just as she reached her arms toward it, the kitten sprang to the top of the woodpile, leaped off it, and sprinted past us.

"Come on!" I urged, forgetting my fear.

We rushed after it. The black-and-white furball streaked down the hall past a side stairwell and closed doors. It jumped over some old paint cans and slowed, but as we caught up, it veered left, nudging a room door open. Camila and I reached the room, panting.

"There's nowhere left to go," I said. For a second I thought, *I should go get Mom.* But what if the kitten ran away before we came back? I didn't want that. We edged inside. The room was crammed with old furniture and boxes stacked almost to the ceiling. I could hear the kitten scuffling around somewhere near the back.

"Let's try to get on either side of it," I whispered to Camila.

She nodded and we split up. I slipped between unsteady-looking towers of boxes, trying not to bump anything. The kitten sounded closer now. I peeked around a corner. Through the maze of boxes, I could see the kitten washing its face with a paw as it perched on a grimy windowsill, A thrill ran through me. *Maybe we could actually catch it!*

Camila was edging in slow motion between two boxes. As she got close to the kitten, I realized I was too far away to get to the other side of it in time. I waved to get Camila's attention, but as I did, the kitten saw Camila—and she lunged for it!

It screeched, jumping for the nearest stack of boxes, and caught the edge of a box, holding on for dear life with its claws.

"Oh NO!" I shrieked, as the kitten clawed its way up the stack of boxes. Camila and I screamed, scrambling to dodge boxes as the stack collapsed and dust and papers rained down. I looked up just in time to see the kitten land nimbly inside a hole at the top of the wall and disappear.

Camila and I stood dazed. Old dusty photographs and papers were everywhere, like piles of dirty snow. "We have to clean this up," I said, surveying the mess.

Camila and I hurried to pick everything up, struggling to lift boxes and stuffing papers back into them. She could tell I was upset, because she said, "Don't worry, it was just an accident." She was right, but I knew it was also our fault.

I gathered some papers and photographs up off the floor and sighed, glancing down at a large black-and-white photo on top. In it, a girl a few years older than me posed by a window in a 1950s-style dress. Her face was heart-shaped, and her shoulder-length blonde hair was swept back in sleek waves. I was about to put the photo into a box with the other papers when I saw something that made me stop, stunned.

"What is it?" asked Camila, but I barely heard her.

Hanging around the girl's neck in the picture was my grandmother Ama's compass necklace.

The Necklace
Chapter 4

I squinted at the photograph of the blonde girl. Although it was faint, I could clearly see the delicate flower design on the compass hanging around her neck. It looked *exactly* like Ama's compass. They were identical.

"What is it? What did you find?" said Camila.

I showed her the photo and explained why I was so surprised. Camila examined the girl's picture. "Do you think this is really your grandmother's necklace?" she asked.

"I don't know," I replied, turning over the bent, dusty photo. On the back, in small, elegant handwriting, were the words "Hallie. July 12, 1956."

"Hallie," I breathed. Questions flooded my brain. Who was Hallie? And why did she have Ama's necklace?

We wove our way back through the maze of
hallways to the Great Room. My mom was talking
to the man in the hard hat at a worktable. Excited,
I showed her the photograph of Hallie.

Mom studied it carefully. "It does look like
Ama's necklace," she admitted, "but I doubt it's the
same one."

"Why not?" I asked.

"It just seems unlikely," she said, sounding tired.

"Well, did Ama ever talk about someone named
Hallie?" I persisted. "Maybe they knew each other."

"I don't think so," Mom said. "Ama never mentioned anyone named Hallie to me, honey. Sorry."

I looked at the photo again. Something about the
way Hallie looked boldly into the camera reminded
me of Ama. "Can I borrow the photo, Mom? We
found it in one of the storage rooms."

My mother thought for a second. Reaching
across to a workstation, she grabbed a clean plastic
bag and put the photo inside. "You can borrow it,"
she said, "as long as you take care of it."

"I promise," I said. She handed the photo to me and I hugged it close, feeling a strange thrill go through me.

At dinner, Camila and I told my parents all about following the kitten and then finding Hallie's photo.

"So you met the Artful Dodger," said Mom.

"That is his name?" asked Camila.

Mom nodded. "He just showed up a few days ago. We think he's living in Coventry House, but we're not quite sure where, mainly because he's so good at running away. That's how Dodger got his name."

"But who owns him?" asked Camila. She looked even more worried when I explained that "stray" meant the Artful Dodger didn't have a family.

"This is terrible!" Camila exclaimed "Lea, we must save Dodger!"

"If you can find him again," my mother noted.

"How was your day?" Dad asked her.

Mom sighed. "Full of the usual problems." She

brushed her hair back from her forehead the way she did when she was worried.

"More funding issues?" asked Dad, concerned. Mom nodded.

"The donor's trying to walk back his initial commitment," she said.

"For Coventry House?" I asked. "I thought you had enough money to restore it."

"Unfortunately, for a project like Coventry House, money is always a challenge," Mom explained. "Restoring historic buildings is expensive, and people often want to tear them down because it's easier and cheaper. They don't think about the fact that these buildings are full of unique details and history that make them irreplaceable. Like Ama's journals," she said to me, "only for a whole community instead of one person. Buildings like Coventry House are part of North St. Louis's identity. They're a big part of the neighborhood's past, and that's worth protecting."

After dinner, I checked my e-mail. Zac had sent

me some photos of the latest animals he'd helped rescue. There were snapshots of a giant armadillo, a monkey with a broken arm, and a pair of baby macaws. The macaws' wrinkled skin made them look like little old men, although parts of their bodies were starting to sprout green and blue feathers, and they had big black eyes. They were so cute! Zac said they'd been been rescued after their mother had disappeared—probably stolen by poachers.

The farther you go into the rainforest, the more poaching is a problem. Poachers kill, trap, and smuggle animals out of the country. We've been working to protect the local populations, but it's not easy. The baby animals we rescue have to be raised by hand at the sanctuary, and even if they can be released back into the wild, they'll be in danger again.

It was inspiring to know how hard my brother was working to protect the animals, but troubling to think of these problems. I told Zac about how Camila and I had found Dodger. *We're going to rescue him, but*

first we have to find him again, I wrote. I considered telling Zac about the photo of Hallie, but I hesitated. It seemed too complicated to tell about in an e-mail, and besides, I didn't really know anything about her. I needed to find out more first.

While Camila brushed her teeth and got ready for bed, I looked at Hallie's photo with my dad's old magnifying glass. Under the magnifying glass, the eight pointed petals were clearly visible on the compass, exactly as they were on Ama's compass.

My grandmother had never told me how she got her necklace. Were there lots of compasses just like this one in St. Louis back when Ama was young? *It can't be just a coincidence,* I thought. *Can it?*

"Maybe tomorrow we can go back to Coventry House and try to catch Dodger," said Camila, coming into my bedroom in her nightgown.

I nodded, still looking at the photo.

"I want to see the big Arch up close. Maybe tomorrow?" Camila said eagerly.

"Don't worry, we'll probably go there for

photography class," I assured her.

I returned to Hallie's photo, searching for clues. Although the photo was black and white, I could tell that Hallie had blonde hair and dark eyes. Her pale dress had an elegant sheen, like silk, and her hands, in short white gloves, rested on a dark sash at her trim waist. Ama's necklace shimmered around her neck, and she had a fresh flower fastened to her bodice with a pin in the shape of a fleur-de-lis.

Hallie stood before a tall window. Its long rectangular panels of glass fitted together in a series of angles that reminded me of a cut crystal's facets. The corners of her mouth turned up in a small, bold smile that made it look like she had a secret. She reminded me of a photo I'd once seen of the old movie star Grace Kelly, poised and perfect.

The longer I looked at the photo, the more questions I had about Hallie—and the more I couldn't wait to start seaching for answers.

The next morning, after we found seats together on the van for our first photography field trip,

# The Necklace

Camila and I told Abby about our discoveries.

"It could be hard to find out anything about Hallie," said Abby. "The photo's so old, and you don't even know her last name."

"I think it'll be fun to figure out who she is!" I said. "Like solving a puzzle."

"We must also rescue Dodger," Camila added.

Abby perked up. "I can help you with that! I always help out at my mom's veterinary clinic when cats get scared. Mom says I'm a cat whisperer." Camila and Abby started talking about cats and how to catch them. "I *know* I can catch Dodger," Abby boasted. "Lea, let's ask your mom if I can come to Coventry House too."

"I'm not sure if we'll be able to visit again," I said. "My mom's really busy there." Camila looked crestfallen.

"Oh, well," said Abby. "So, Camila, what else do you want to do while you're here?"

Camila lit up. "I want to see the Mississippi River, and the Arch . . . "

"You haven't been to the Arch yet?" said Abby, amazed. "You *have* to go there! And you have to go

to Six Flags, and Grant's Farm, and City Museum—oh, and you need to try frozen custard from Ted Drewes. It's the most delicious thing on earth. Right, Lea?"

I nodded. I was going to add that we needed to find Hallie first, but Abby kept talking about frozen custard until the van rolled to a stop.

Ms. Garcia stood up in the aisle. "Okay, photographers!" she chirped. "Welcome to our first urban exploration. Today we're going to be taking pictures of the Soulard Market. Some of you may have been here before, but that's okay—if you're paying attention, you can always find something new to look at, even in a place you know well."

I recognized the pretty redbrick building in front of us. "This market," Ms. Garcia told us, "has been here for more than a century, so there are plenty of interesting things to photograph."

We followed Ms. Garcia up to the arched front entrance and through the double doors. Inside, endless rows of stalls filled the hall, displaying fresh vegetables, meats, fruits, and flowers. "Please stay inside the market area," Ms. Garcia called after us.

 The Necklace

"We'll meet at the front entrance in thirty minutes. Have fun!"

The class spread out, cameras poised. Camila headed down an aisle, snapping pictures, with Abby a few steps behind her.

I stood still, remembering what Ms. Garcia had told us about trying to see in a new way. I looked around and then took a few photos of oranges piled in a pyramid. But when I checked my shots, they all looked sort of dull. The last thing I wanted to hear was Ms. Garcia saying that I'd taken another boring photo.

I glanced around again. Camila and Abby had disappeared into the sea of shoppers. For a moment, I felt nervous and wondered if I should go try to find them. Yet a voice inside me said, *No. Focus on what's in front of you.* It sounded like something Ama would say. I took a deep, calming breath and slowly made my way down an aisle, making sure I didn't miss anything.

I'd been coming to Soulard Market with my family a few times a year ever since I could remember. Still, as I raised my camera up and looked

through the lens, I began noticing things I hadn't seen before, like how the sunlight streamed onto the polished, swirly gray-green floor, and how the iron lampposts at the end of each row of stalls were standing guard. I started snapping photographs, trying to capture the images.

I turned a corner. At the end of the next aisle was a bright stall with a yellow-and-pink-striped awning. The Flaky Bakery was one of Ama's favorite shops. We would go there whenever we came to the market together. Sadness washed over me like an ocean wave. For a brief moment, I could almost see Ama there, nose pressed to the cupcake display, her compass necklace swinging. "Vanilla with chocolate frosting?" she'd ask me, "or chocolate with vanilla?" Then, before I could answer, she'd say, "Why choose? Let's have both." Just thinking about it made me smile.

I stepped up to the display case. Pastel cupcakes stood in neat rows behind the gleaming glass, their pink, blue, and lavender whipped-frosting tops making them look like sugary spring flowers. Without thinking, I lifted my camera and focused on the

colorful cupcakes, zooming closer as I shot. Happiness bloomed inside me. Taking photos always made me feel better.

I didn't realize I'd spent a half hour shooting cupcakes, but when I checked the wall clock, it was time to meet the class. As I came out the front doors, our van was by the curb and Abby and Camila were comparing shots nearby.

Camila saw me first. "Did you see the horses? They were huge!" she blurted.

"Clydesdales, they were Clydesdales!" said Abby, as they both rushed over. Abby showed me a few photos of Camila petting a team of draft horses yoked to a wagon, laughing, and even kissing one of their noses.

"I can't believe you missed them!" Abby said. She and Camila kept talking about the horses, noting how huge but gentle they were, and how soft. Excitedly, they showed me the rest of their photos. Most were of Camila or Abby making faces for the camera and having fun. All their shots were bursting with life. By comparison, my photos seemed dull.

"What did you photograph, Lea?" Camila asked.

"Just some cupcakes," I said. I waited for them to ask to see my pictures, but they didn't.

✦

Camila and Abby sat together on the way back. I was one seat behind them next to Kevin, who wanted to show me all the photos he'd taken of the sausages at Eddie's Meats. "Sweet apple, sun-dried tomato, spinach feta," he said proudly, clicking through his photos. It seemed as if he had taken a million of them. "Italian is my favorite. But look at this one ... and this one ... "

I nodded politely as I tried to overhear what Camila and Abby were talking about.

"I love horses," Camila was saying. "In Brazil, you can ride them on the beach!"

"That sounds so fun," said Abby. "I *have* to come visit you now!"

"Yes!" Camila agreed, sounding happy. I caught a snippet of Abby telling her how she'd taught her dog to play soccer before I finally gave up trying to eavesdrop and started looking at my photos. Cup-cakes. Lots of cupcakes.

Kevin leaned over. "Hey," he said, appraising my shots. "Looks like you like cupcakes as much as I love sausages!"

I gave him a weak smile.

Once we got out of the van at COCA, Abby ran up to me. "Hey, Lea, would you mind if Camila came over after camp today?"

"If your dad says it's okay," added Camila.

"We want to play soccer in my backyard," Abby bubbled. She turned to Camila. "I have a net and everything. And you can help feed Tiny—he's the newborn puppy my mom is fostering. I'll ask her, but now that he's getting bigger, I'm sure she'll say it's okay."

I felt a sharp pang of jealousy. I'd been *begging* Abby to let me help feed Tiny, or even *hold* him. All I'd been allowed to do so far was look at him in his shoebox.

"Lea," said Abby, "I know you're not into soccer, so I don't know if you want to come, but you can if you want."

"I can't," I said curtly. "I have to go through Ama's journals to see if she mentioned Hallie."

Abby looked confused. "Can't you do that another time?"

I shook my head. "I should do it soon, before I have to return the photograph."

I was hoping that either Camila or Abby would offer to help, but Abby just shrugged. "Okay," she said, adding, "We'll miss you."

"Yes," Camila said. I could tell they were trying to be kind, but somehow that didn't make me feel any better.

That afternoon, while Dad was taking Camila to Abby's house, I dug out Ama's travel journals. Mom had put most of Ama's mementos in boxes in the attic, but I'd kept the journals in my bookcase after we got home from Brazil. Now, I stacked the four worn leather books on the window seat, curled up on the old velvet cushion, and started to read. The first time I'd opened my grandmother's journals, on the plane ride to Brazil, I had read them for hours. But today it was hard to stay focused. I kept thinking about how much fun Camila and Abby were probably having,

even when I reminded myself that they were just playing soccer while I was searching for important clues about Hallie and the compass necklace.

Ama's first journal started in 1996. She talked about all the adventures she was having in Hawaii and then Bali. Even though I'd read it before, it was still interesting. Unfortunately, she didn't talk about her past at all, and there was no mention of anyone named Hallie. After reading for over an hour, I started to wonder if this was a waste of time. Mid-way through the second journal, Ama was traveling through Siberia on a bicycling trip. She described stopping for lunch by a field of irises:

> *They reminded me (of course!) of St. Louis, of my favorite flower, copper irises, and my compass necklace, and of that promise I made when I was sixteen—and how far I've come since then.*

I sat up. *That promise I made when I was sixteen—* What was she talking about? Ama had never told me of any special promises she had made involving her compass necklace. To whom had she made a

promise? Could it have been Hallie? And *what* had she promised? Whatever it was, the promise must have been very important for her to remember it so many years later.

I read the rest of the journal as fast as I could, looking for any mention of Hallie or the compass necklace, but there was nothing else. There was no mention of them in the third journal, either. By the time I started the last one, my eyes were tired from staring at the pages, but I kept going. Finally, I got to where my own diary entries started. I turned to the most recent entry.

CAMILA IS ARRIVING AND I AM SO EXCITED! Can you tell? :) I can't wait to see her again, and show her all the great things about St. Louis!

Reading those words now suddenly made me feel a little sad.

I looked up. Hickory Street was dark outside the window. I'd missed the chance to spend an afternoon with Camila, and I still had no idea how I was going to find Hallie.

The Jewel Box

Chapter 5

When Camila and I got to COCA the next morning, Ms. Garcia was already waiting with the rest of the class by the van.

Abby rushed up as we approached. "Guess what? We're going to take pictures at Forest Park today!" she said.

Excitement raced through me. Forest Park is one of the best parts of St. Louis. It's huge and packed with a zillion things to see, like the planetarium and the zoo. "Maybe we'll go to Turtle Playground," I told Camila. "They have these giant cement turtle sculptures. Hey, they're sort of like the big wooden turtle sculptures at the sea turtle sanctuary in Praia Tropical!"

Camila nodded, her eyes lit with recognition. She lived in Praia Tropical, so she'd been to Amigos

do Oceano, the sea turtle sanctuary, many times.

Abby popped up behind us. "You have to see the Muny!" she said to Camila, as we climbed into the van. "It's this big theater that puts on free musicals in the summer, and we all go and watch and eat a picnic dinner. It's so much fun."

When we took our seats, Abby started telling Camila all about the Muny. I noticed that Camila had done her hair in two high mini buns, just like Abby. I pulled my backpack onto my knees. Inside, in a folder wrapped carefully in a plastic bag, was the photo of Hallie. I'd brought it with me to show Abby, but somehow it seemed awkward to mention it right now, especially when Abby started taking pictures of Camila and making her laugh.

Before I knew it, the van pulled up to the park's main entrance. Ms. Garcia turned around in the front seat to face us. "Okay, photographers!" she said, grinning. "Forest Park is one of the best places to take pictures in St. Louis, and today we'll be visiting my all-time favorite spot, so make sure you're paying attention."

We followed Ms. Garcia into the park. Rolling

green lawn stretched out so far in front of us,
I couldn't see where it ended. Ms. Garcia moved
quickly down one path and across to another. Soon
we were approaching the World's Fair Pavilion, with
its tumbling stone waterfall in front.

"Is that where we're going?" Kevin asked.
Ms. Garcia just smiled and shook her head.

We passed a glassy lake outlined by purple-leaf
plum trees. On a tiny island in the center stood
Forest Park's circular bandstand. With its elaborate
details and blue-green copper dome, it reminded me
of a frozen carousel. I remembered seeing it a few
summers ago with Abby, when we went to an out-
door performance of *The Wizard of Oz* at the Muny.
I was about to remind Abby about it, but when I
looked around, she and Camila were far away.

The path crested up steeply, and we panted,
struggling to get to the top. As we did, another
building came into view, glittering in the sunlight.
Except for a few metal bars and a stone entrance, it
looked like it was made entirely of glass. I had to
run to catch up to Camila and Abby.

"Ladies and gentlemen," Ms. Garcia said

dramatically, "welcome to the St. Louis Floral Conservatory, also known as the Jewel Box."

"It *does* look like a jewel box," whispered Camila, and she was right. The building's tiers of windows, stair-stepping roof, and metal double doors seemed like an elaborate case for treasures. The closer we got, the more light bounced off the glass, until it felt like we were walking into a giant diamond. I'd been here before, and every time I saw it again, I had the same reaction—I wanted to take a picture.

Inside, colorful spring flowers like roses, lilies, and daffodils overflowed long beds and crowded displays. I stopped to breathe in the sweet perfume. A tour guide with steel-gray hair swept up in a tight bun introduced herself. She motioned for us to follow her down the center aisle as she told us about the building.

"Since it was completed in 1936, the Jewel Box has become one of the world's most famous decorative greenhouses," she lectured. "At any given time, hundreds of rare and ornamental plants are on display, none of which are to be touched—*ever*." She gave us all a stern look to make her point.

 The Jewel Box

Ms. Garcia stepped up. "Yes! Thank you! I know my students are going to be very respectful," she said brightly. "Now, guys," said Ms. Garcia, turning to us, "the Jewel Box and these plants were *made* to be photographed. With all the natural light and beautiful flowers, it's impossible to take a bad picture here. So relax, let your imaginations run wild, and *keep seeing in a new way.*"

I looked around. The class was scattering fast. Abby and Camila were already snapping shots of the clusters of ruby tulips lining the long center fountain. As they leaned their heads together, I couldn't help admiring their matching mini buns. When Abby said something to Camila that I couldn't hear, they broke into giggles. I pulled out my camera, trying to ignore the feeling of being left out.

Above me, sunlight streamed through the line of glass windows. I snapped some shots of sunbeams hitting a wall of climbing roses, but when I checked the camera, the roses looked washed-out. Frustrated, I moved down the path, back toward the front entrance. On my right was a space where several long, rectangular glass windows met in a corner.

I paused. Looking at it gave me a strange feeling—it looked familiar, but I didn't know why. At first it made me think of the square, cut-glass crystal vase my mom sometimes puts flowers in. Then it hit me: *It looked like the background of Hallie's photo.*

I unzipped my backpack, pulled out the photo, and compared it with the real-life corner in front of me. Sure enough, Hallie was standing in her silk dress, wearing the compass necklace, in front of the *exact spot* I was looking at.

This is where Hallie's photo was taken! I nearly burst with excitement.

Camila and Abby were a little confused when I raced up, blathering, "Hallie! The photo! It happened here! You guys have to come, quick!" Neither seemed that interested until I showed them the photo side by side with the corner and they saw what I saw.

"This was definitely taken here," said Abby, studying the photo.

Camila looked at me, her eyes shining. "What should we do now, Lea?"

"We need to find out *why* Hallie was here," I said.

I wasn't sure if the grumpy tour guide could help me, but she was the only person I could think of to ask.

She was intrigued by the photograph. "Yes," she said, looking at the date on the back. "This photo was taken here. The Jewel Box hosted frequent debutante balls throughout 1956."

"*Deb-you-tante?*" asked Camila, confused. "What is that?"

"Several decades ago, wealthy families in St. Louis would hold a ball, or dance, where girls turning sixteen would enter society," said the tour guide.

Abby frowned. "I don't understand," she said.

"I don't either," I admitted. "Aren't they already *in* society?"

"Not *officially*," replied the tour guide, letting go of an impatient sigh.

Now I was even more confused. Judging from their expressions, so were Camila and Abby.

"What does it mean, 'in society'?" asked Camila.

Exasperated, the tour guide turned to Ms. Garcia,

who'd been listening from a few feet away.

"At that time, 'society' was a word used to mean wealthy and well-known families in the city," Ms. Garcia told us. She came over and looked at the photograph of Hallie, glancing at the note on the back. "In 1956, women didn't have the same opportunities to be educated or pursue careers that we have now. A debutante ball was where well-to-do young ladies were formally introduced to young men," she said, adding, "In some families, girls were expected to simply look pretty and get married. Hallie may have done that."

I felt a flash of stubborn annoyance. "I don't think so," I said. Looking at the compass—and the way Hallie boldly stared at the camera—reminded me again of Ama somehow. "I think Hallie wanted to travel and explore," I said.

Ms. Garcia looked amused. "How do you know that?" she said.

"It's just a hunch," I replied. "Also, she's wearing my grandmother Ama's compass necklace."

"It *looks* like Ama's compass," said Abby, "but it might not be the same exact one. Maybe they both just bought it at the same store, separately."

I knew Abby could be right. Still, it bothered me to hear her say it. I might not have been able to prove it, but I felt sure it was Ama's compass. Wasn't that enough for Abby to believe me?

We all stared at the photo. My eyes fell on the flower pinned to Hallie's dress. It was shaped like a lily, but smaller, and its six long petals stood out from one another like a star.

"What's this called?" I asked, pointing to it. "That's called a corsage," said Ms. Garcia.

"No, I mean what kind of flower is it?" I said.

The tour guide squinted at the photo. "It's hard to tell since the photo is in black and white, but from the size and shape I'd say it's a copper iris."

The name made my heart stop. Just last night in Ama's journal, I'd read that copper irises were her favorite kind of flower! *That can't be a coincidence*, I thought.

"They're native to Missouri," the guide went on. "They're small, but they have a very distinct appearance, quite unique—like this." She walked us to another area of the greenhouse and pointed to a

clump of irises growing beside a small fountain. The blossoms were much smaller than the yellow and purple flag irises I was used to seeing at this time of year, and their color was unusual and striking, coppery-red with gold accents.

"I want to find out who Hallie is," I told her.

"If I were you," said the guide, "I'd go look in the city archives at the main library downtown. That's where we keep all of our historical papers for the Floral Conservatory. If an event was held here on July 12, 1956, they might have a record of it."

Over dinner that night, Camila and I told my parents the latest chapter in what I was now calling "The Hunt for Hallie."

"It sounds like you two had an interesting day," my dad said as he scooped mashed potatoes onto his plate.

"It was more than just *interesting*, Dad," I said. "This is important new information! Maybe Ama and Hallie were debutantes together?"

"I don't think so." Mom took a bite of salad.

She hadn't said much during my retelling of the day's adventures.

"Why not?" I asked. "Maybe Ama was at the Jewel Box that night, too!"

"Honey, there's no way Ama was a debutante," my mother said. "Her parents wouldn't have had the money to pay for an expensive dress. They were immigrants. Anyway, they didn't believe in that type of thing. They would have thought it was frivolous."

"What does 'frivolous' mean?" asked Camila.

"Silly, or wasteful," said my mother. "Besides, by the summer of 1956, my grandfather—Ama's father—had already moved the whole family out of St. Louis to West County," Mom went on. "Ama was working at the family grocery store and studying. She wasn't going to debutante balls. I think the whole necklace thing is just a coincidence."

"Well, it still can't hurt to go to the library tomorrow and check," I said, persisting.

When the phone in the hall rang, Dad went to answer it. He returned looking surprised.

"It's for you, Camila," he said. "It's Abby."

Abby? Calling for *Camila* and not me? Hurt

feelings welled in my throat, but I tried not to show them. Instead, I studied my peas and pork chops while Camila talked on the phone. When she came back in, her eyes were sparkling.

"Abby invited me to go with her to a baseball game!" Camila said. "Yesterday I mentioned that I would like to see the St. Louis Cardinals play, and Abby's father has an extra ticket for tomorrow!"

"That's fantastic!" Dad said. "You have to go."

"Of course you do," said Mom. "It'll be a memorable experience. You girls will have so much fun!"

"Yes," Camila said, looking at me nervously, "but Abby says her father has only one extra ticket."

I bit my lip.

"That's okay," Dad said, trying to smooth over the awkwardness. "You're not the biggest sports fan anyway, are you, Lea?"

I shrugged, looking down at my plate.

"While you two are at the game, Lea and I can hit the library," Dad continued, "and resume The Hunt for Hallie."

Camila looked at me, concerned. "Are you sure, Lea?"

I wasn't, actually. It's true that I don't love sports, but I *also* didn't love the idea of Camila and Abby having a fun time without me. I realized with surprise that I was a little jealous that Abby had asked Camila and not me. Still, I didn't want to make Camila feel bad. So instead I said, "You should go. You'll have a great time."

Camila smiled with relief.

I smiled back at her. But inside I still felt awful.

The Library

Chapter 6

Dear Journal,

It's past my bedtime, but I can't sleep. I keep thinking about Camila and Abby. They're getting along so well, which is great, because they're both my friends. So why don't I feel more excited that they want to spend time together?

Normally when I have a problem I talk to Abby. But I can't talk to her about this!

Sometimes Zac has good advice, but with everything that he's dealing with in Brazil, I don't want to bother him. I'm worried about Zac. Part of me wishes he would come home, but I know he's working to protect the animals. Still, I don't like

thinking about him being in any kind of danger.

Since I can't talk to anyone about Abby and Camila, I'm going to focus on finding out more about Hallie. I just can't shake the feeling that there's some link between Hallie and Ama.

"Look alive, Lea," my dad teased. I was lagging behind as we climbed the wide marble front steps to the Central Library entrance. We go to our local library a lot, but we hadn't come downtown to the main branch in a while. I'd forgotten how huge the elegant granite building was . . . and how many steps it had!

"What floor are the archives on again?" I asked, out of breath, as we moved through the entrance.

"Fourth," he replied.

"Is there an elevator?"

"We don't need an elevator! You climbed a mountain in Brazil—twice in one day, remember?" Dad said. "Besides, it's great therapy for my leg," he added.

"What's an archive, anyway?" I asked, panting a bit as we scaled the last flight of stairs.

"It's a place that keeps historical records and papers," he explained. "The records can't be checked out like library books, but people can still visit to look at them."

It sounded sort of like a museum, but when we reached the archive, its low light and leather chairs reminded me more of a cozy study. Unfortunately, when my father told the archive librarian what we needed, her smile faded.

"I'm so sorry," she said regretfully. "Our records for the Floral Conservatory don't begin until 1982. A storage fire destroyed everything before that. You're welcome to look at any of the other photos and records we have," she added, maybe because I looked so disappointed.

"Is there anything else that you want to look at while we're here, Lea?" Dad asked.

"Do you have any old photos of Coventry House?" I asked the librarian. "That's where we found Hallie's photo," I told her. "Maybe there's a clue there."

We sat at a polished dark wood table. Soon, the librarian brought over several boxes full of antique photos, each covered in protective plastic. Carefully, Dad and I sifted through them. There were sepia pictures of Coventry House being built, with Francis Coventry posing proudly on the front steps, with his daughters in a horse-drawn carriage out front. Dad found a long photo of a large group of children sitting on the front steps, from when the house was an orphanage. There were even a few photos from after the house had been abandoned, with its windows broken. They were all interesting, but none of them offered any clue about Hallie.

And yet her photo had been stored at Coventry House, so there had to be a connection. Could Hallie possibly have been a granddaughter of Francis Coventry's? It didn't seem very likely that she was an orphan.

I turned over a big photo. Unlike most of the other pictures of Coventry House, this one was in color. I could tell it was spring from the buds on the trees. The blue sky was bright behind the turrets, but what caught my attention were the tall rust-colored

flowers lining the neat path to the front door. I knew instantly what they were.

"Copper irises!" I said, excitement making my voice loud. The librarian shot us a glance. I lowered my voice and leaned toward Dad.

"Copper irises were Ama's favorite flower. And Hallie wore one as a corsage in her photo!" I told him.

"Okay," Dad said, looking a little confused. "So what does that mean?"

I have no idea, I realized. "I don't know, but it means *something,*" I insisted stubbornly. Somehow Hallie, Ama, the compass necklace, and the irises were all connected, I felt sure of it. I just had to figure out how.

On the way home, I tried to think of ways Hallie and Ama could have known each other. "Maybe they were both gardeners?" I said.

Dad chuckled. "I don't think so," he replied. "Your grandmother had many talents, but she did not have a green thumb."

I sighed, slumping back in my seat.

"Keep going," Dad encouraged me. "A true explorer doesn't give up if things aren't going well."

I knew he was right, but now that the excitement of discovering the photo of irises at Coventry House had worn off, I was feeling a little discouraged. As I looked out the window, my thoughts drifted from Hallie and Ama to Abby and Camila at the baseball game. They were probably eating popcorn and frozen custard and laughing at jokes that they wouldn't remember to tell me. Suddenly, my copper iris discovery didn't seem so important.

"How do you like having Camila here?" Dad asked.

I was startled. Normally Mom's the one with the freaky ability to read my mind, not Dad.

"Um . . . it's okay," I said.

"Just okay?" he said.

"It's different from what I expected," I added after a moment.

Dad considered this. "You know, in my experience, when something's different from what you expect, it can sometimes turn out to be even *better*

79

than you expected—as long as you keep an open mind about it."

"Okay," I said, and turned on the radio to fill the awkward silence. I didn't really want to talk with him about it. I was already trying not to think about it.

As we pulled into our driveway, Camila ran out to meet us. I barely recognized her. "STL" was painted on her cheeks in red and white, and she was wearing a Cardinals baseball cap and waving a big red foam finger that said "#1" on it. Her face flushed with happiness.

Mom had to work late, so we ordered pizza. Over dinner, Camila told me and Dad how she and Abby had gotten their faces painted at Busch Stadium, and sat behind home plate and done the wave every time St. Louis scored. Plus, the guy next to them caught a foul ball, and gave it to Camila when he found out she was visiting from Brazil. It sounded a lot more fun than my day.

Camila turned to me. "Did you learn anything

new about Hallie at the library?"

"Not really," I said, picking a mushroom off my pizza and nibbling it.

"Hey, that's not quite true," said Dad. He told Camila about the photo of the irises outside Coventry House.

"It is another clue!" Camila said enthusiastically. "I am sure you will find Hallie!"

"I hope so," I replied, trying to share her confidence. *Maybe the problem is that I'm trying to do this on my own,* I thought. It was always more inspiring— and more fun—to have a partner. I turned to Camila, but just as I was about to ask if she and Abby could help me, Camila remembered that it was time for her to video-chat with her cousin Paloma in Brazil.

Twenty minutes later, she was still in front of the computer screen, shaking the #1 finger at Paloma and talking animatedly in Portuguese. *I'll ask her tomorrow,* I told myself, but as I climbed the stairs, I felt more discouraged than ever.

My journal was lying on the bed. I picked it up and then got under the covers, burrowing in. I fished a pen out of my nightstand and started

writing. I didn't even write "Dear Journal." I just put down everything I was feeling in that moment.

Maybe I'll never figure out who Hallie was. And Camila and Abby might not even want to help me at all. They're too busy having fun without me.

I turned my head. On the nightstand was one of my favorite photos of Ama, beaming with a Masai guide in front of Mount Kilimanjaro in Kenya. Her face shone with confidence. I longed to talk to her. I knew she would understand. Usually, looking at that photo made me happy, but this time all I could see was how far away Ama seemed.

City Museum

Chapter 7

On our way to camp the next morning, Dad mentioned he'd be giving Abby a ride to our house after camp. "Her mom has to work late at the veterinary clinic, and her dad's at a conference," he explained. "Besides, I figured you three girls would want to hang out after camp anyway. This way, you don't have to waste time asking if Abby can come over," he added with a wink.

I smiled, but inside I felt a twinge of worry. Ever since Camila arrived, things between Abby and me had been kind of odd. I was glad that the two of them were hitting it off, but when Abby had invited Camila to go to the Cardinals game with her, she hadn't even bothered to check if I wanted to come, too. Just thinking about that hurt my feelings all over again.

I was hoping I'd get a moment to talk to Abby about it on our own before camp started, but when Dad rolled into the parking lot, everyone except us was already boarding the class van. After we got in, Ms. Garcia told the class we were going to City Museum. We all got really excited, except for Camila, who looked curious.

"What is City Museum?" she asked.

"The MOST amazingly weird place in all of St. Louis," I told her. "Possibly in the *world*," added Abby.

We looked at each other knowingly, and for that brief moment I felt close to her again.

When we got to the museum, Camila finally understood what we meant. There is nothing subtle about City Museum, from the school bus teetering on the edge of the roof, to the giant crane with two half-finished airplanes hanging from it next to a medieval stone tower—and that's just *outside*! Inside it's even crazier. There's the 10 Story Slide made of old metal mail chutes that spirals from the top floor of the building all the way down to the ground. For those unafraid of heights, there are twisting metal

tunnels that extend across the building in midair for people to climb through. Camila paled when she saw those.

More to her liking were the caves covered in broken mirror pieces, and signs directing you to "The World's Largest Underpants!" The whole place is like someone's hyper imagination exploded into reality.

As the class headed through the lobby, everyone kept bumping into one another as we tried to take in everything at once. "This entire museum is a work of art," Ms. Garcia told us. "Almost everything you see has been thrown away, then rediscovered and given new life as part of a ride or exhibit." Her eyes sparkled as she looked around. "City Museum itself is the definition of seeing the world in a new way, so it should be easy for you to take some unique photographs here."

We had forty-five minutes to take pictures. I headed to the roof. Beside the school bus hanging off the roof's edge, there was a giant dome, and an old-fashioned Ferris wheel. I was trying to capture the color and action around me—like the excited kids and adults running around discovering creativity at every

turn. Here, the impossible seemed totally normal.

I spent a lot of time waiting for the right moment to take pictures. After half a dozen shots, I scrolled back through my pictures. There were some good details, but none of them really captured the rush of energy I felt. Instead, they just looked jumbled, like I didn't know what I wanted to photograph. It was frustrating. I didn't feel like I was "seeing in a new way" at all.

I came back inside, disappointed. Camp would be ending in a few days. If I didn't improve, maybe it was a sign that I wasn't really that good at photography after all. Who had I been trying to kid?

My eyes drifted across the room. Camila was standing alone by the entrance to the 10 Story Slide, watching kids walk in.

"Camila!" I said. "What are you doing up here?"

"Oh, Lea," she said, looking happy to see me. "Abby is insisting that I go down the slide, because it is the most fun thing to do here. But when I went to the entrance and looked down . . . " She shivered. "Abby has already gone down," she said, twisting her long hair tightly around a finger. "I want to go

too, but I don't think I can do it."

"Sure you can!" I said. "Once you start, it goes really fast, so you'll be at the bottom before you know it. Besides, being a *little* scared is part of what makes it fun." I was trying to reassure her, but she looked even more anxious. "You know what my grandmother Ama always said?" I added, hoping to encourage her. "She said, 'I'm not fearless, but I don't let my fears *stop* me.' Camila, if you really want to go down the slide, don't let being afraid stop you."

"Your grandmother was brave," Camila said, but her eyes still looked worried.

"Do you want me to go with you?" I offered.

Camila looked surprised, and then she nodded. "Yes!" she said, adding, "But you go in front."

The entrance to the 10 Story Slide was steep, and when I peered in, all I could see was blackness twisting downward. I sat down, and Camila sat behind me, hugging my waist with both hands. In the distance, we could hear the echo of kids screaming with frightened delight as they wound their way down toward the bottom. For a second, I wished I could see what was ahead, and I felt a delicious

tingle of fear. I turned and glanced back at Camila.
Her eyes were squeezed tightly closed. Suddenly
I had an idea. Pulling out my camera, I told Camila
I was going to take some pictures as we went down.

"Okay," she said, her eyes still clamped shut.

"Ready?" I asked. Camila nodded and gripped
my shoulders hard. "One, two, THREE!" I shouted,
and we launched ourselves down the slide.

Metal spun by above me. Camila was shrieking,
but she sounded more thrilled than afraid. As the
sides of the slide flew by, I held my camera in front
of me and pressed the shutter button down and held
it, so burst mode kicked in. I looked upside down at
Camila, and took a photo of her screaming and
laughing at the same time. I kept pressing the button
until we flew out the end of the slide and onto some
giant beanbags, breathless.

Camila went down the slide three more times
after our first ride, all by herself. "They must build
one just like it in Brazil!" she exclaimed as the van
pulled away from City Museum. It made me feel
warm inside to think that I'd helped Camila face
her fear of heights.

I felt even better when I started looking through the photographs I'd taken on the slide. Most of the shots were blurry or showed nothing but darkness, since the slide was a tunnel of metal twists and turns, but one photo was a strange combination of Camila's face and the darkness surrounding her. The camera flash made Camila's eyes shine in a spooky way, and her expression was a jumble of joy and fear. I'd never taken a photo that looked like that before. That afternoon, Ms. Garcia taught us how to crop photos, fix red-eye, airbrush, and shift color in Photoshop. She walked around as we worked at our computers, looking at our pictures and offering suggestions. When she saw the photo I'd taken of Camila on the slide, she stopped.

"Wow," she said. "You were *on* the slide when you took that?"

I nodded.

Ms. Garcia folded her arms, impressed. "So did the photo turn out the way you expected?"

"I didn't really know what to expect," I confessed. "I think that's why I like it so much."

"That's a great thing to realize," Ms. Garcia said,

nodding. "Sometimes the best photographs we take come from experimenting, and not being afraid to try new ways of using the camera. This photograph shows real creativity, Lea. You approached taking the photo in a new way, and you really captured all the emotions people feel when they go down the slide.

"Not only that, but your photo made *me* feel fear and joy, too. Keep it up," she said, and gave me a pat on the shoulder. I felt tingly and happy as she walked off. Maybe by "seeing in a new way," Ms. Garcia wasn't talking about what was in front of my eyes, but how I thought about what I saw. In any case, I felt like I'd made a breakthrough. Now, if only I could somehow have a breakthrough and figure out the mystery of Hallie.

After class, Abby, Camila, and I waited outside COCA for Dad to pick us up. Abby pulled out a piece of scratch paper, crumpled it up, and started bouncing it on her knees, practicing her soccer moves. I watched for a few minutes. I had been waiting most of the day for Abby to ask me how my search for Hallie was going, but she still hadn't, so I decided to mention it.

"Um, so, I was thinking we could go back to the archives and look through their photos for Hallie," I suggested. "Maybe we can find something new."

Abby shrugged and kept bouncing the paper ball on her knees. It was getting sort of annoying. "Maybe," she said, passing the paper ball to Camila using the side of her foot.

Camila bounced it back. "I think we should go to Coventry House," she said. "We can see Dodger."

"Yes!" Abby chimed in. She kicked the paper ball back to Camila. "That's what we should do!"

"I don't think we have time," I said as I watched them pass the ball back and forth. "We need to work on finding Hallie."

"We can do that another day," said Abby, without looking at me. "Let's ask your dad to take us to Coventry House. Then I can use my cat-whispering skills to save Dodger."

I felt myself getting upset. Abby wasn't listening to me. Neither was Camila, because she clapped her hands and said, "Yes!" She turned to me. "Lea, will you ask your dad?"

I shrugged. I didn't want to be mean, but I *really* wanted to keep trying to find Hallie. "Does it have to be today?" I asked.

Abby caught her paper ball and turned to me. "Of course it does! Dodger is a *stray*. At any moment he could be hurt or run over. He needs our help."

She said it as if I didn't *want* to help Dodger, which bothered me even more. "Abby, just because you *think* you can get Dodger to come to you doesn't mean you *will*."

Abby crossed her arms over her chest, the way she does whenever someone tells her she can't do something. "Just because you're trying to find Hallie doesn't mean *you* will," she retorted.

I gasped. It felt as if she'd just pushed me, hard. I looked from Abby to Camila, who was watching with round eyes. "That was mean," I said, my voice quavering.

Abby uncrossed her arms. "I just meant that it's kind of a long shot," she said more softly.

"What do you think, Camila?" I asked.

Camila looked from Abby to me. "I am not sure," she said uncomfortably.

I felt my lower lip start to tremble. I'd been hoping Camila would defend me, but I could see that wasn't going to happen.

"Lea, why are you upset?" asked Camila. She looked worried.

"Yes, why?" asked Abby, which just made it worse. Suddenly everything I'd been feeling and wanting to say for the last few days started to rush through me—and spilled out of my mouth before I could stop it.

"I know you guys don't care about finding Hallie," I said. "I can tell you just want to play soccer and go to Cardinals games and eat frozen custard and have fun without me."

Both looked startled. "That's not true," Abby said, but I cut her off.

"Yes, it is," I said, feeling tears starting.

"No, it's not," insisted Camila, "but all *you* want to do is look for Hallie."

"What?!" I asked, feeling defensive.

Camila twisted her hair. "You said we were going to explore St. Louis *together*—but I don't think you really want to explore *with* me. You don't want to

go back to Coventry House, or visit the Arch or the Mississippi River ... "

"I've been to those places!" I said.

"*I* haven't," Camila said, almost apologetically. "You say you want to be an explorer, Lea, but you only want to explore the things you want, not what anyone else wants."

"That's not true!" I shouted.

My face felt like it was burning up. Before anyone could say anything else, I turned my back on them and hurried toward COCA, breaking into a run so they wouldn't see the hot tears spill down my cheeks.

The Mural in the Morning Room
Chapter 8

I locked myself in a stall in the lobby bathroom and cried. It didn't make me feel much better. Taking a deep breath, I thought about the last few days and how I'd acted with Camila. I remembered how she'd kept mentioning going to see the Arch, or Dodger—and how I'd brushed her off. I felt awful when I realized that I had been thinking so much about finding Hallie, I'd forgotten to be a good host to Camila. She was only here for a week, and I hadn't been listening to her at all! No wonder Camila was having more fun with Abby.

After a few minutes, Abby knocked softly on the bathroom door and told me my dad was there to pick us up. We walked to the station wagon in awkward silence. No one spoke once we got into the car, but if Dad noticed anything was wrong, he didn't mention

95

it. Instead, as he pulled out of the parking lot, he said, "We need to swing by Coventry House, girls. I have to drop something off for Lea's mom."

Camila perked up. "We can see Dodger!" she said to Abby. Even though I didn't smile with them, the thought of maybe petting a kitten made me feel a little better, too.

"*This* is Coventry House?" exclaimed Abby when we pulled up outside the old mansion my mom was restoring. "It's like a castle," she whispered. By the time we passed through the main entrance into the front hall with its curving double staircase, Abby's eyes were wide with wonder.

"Dad," I asked, "can we show Abby around?"

"Sure," he said, "but only if it's a quick tour. I need you to be back here, ready to go in fifteen minutes." We nodded, and he disappeared into the Great Room.

Camila walked around the main entry area, checking all the nooks. "I don't see Dodger," she said, letting go of a huge sigh.

"It's a big building," I replied. "And he's a cat—he could be anywhere."

Camila nodded and sat down next to Abby at the base of the double staircase. Abby looked sad. For a moment, I forgot that we were in a fight. I just wanted Abby to see some of what made Coventry House so unique.

"Hey," I said to her, "do you want to see something?"

Abby's face lit up when Camila and I showed her the hidden door by the foyer. "Whoa," she said. "A secret room!"

"It's a morning room," I told her, "and it has a hidden mural they're restoring. Want to see?"

Abby nodded eagerly.

The minute we walked in, it was obvious things had changed. A few days ago, the mural had been covered in cloudy plaster. Now, the wall it was on was exploding with color: swirling purples, golds, bronzes, and blues.

Sarah the art restorer was standing on a ladder nearby with a small tray of water, dabbing part of the wall with a wet cloth. Seeing us, she waved and took

out her earbuds. "Hey there! What do you think?" she asked.

"It looks incredible!" I exclaimed. Sarah grinned.

As we got closer, she stepped off the ladder and pushed it back, exposing the full mural. Beneath the painting's bright blue sky and whirling cloud were three girls in a field of flowers, wearing identical, old-fashioned dresses with wide square collars and knee-length skirts. One held an open book in her lap, another stood playing the violin, and a third danced. The wind blew back their dresses and hair in waves, and the field they stood in was full of ruddy, star-shaped flowers that I immediately recognized.

"*Copper irises!*" I whispered.

Sarah tilted her head at me. "How'd you know that?" she asked.

Abby and Camila's eyes were round with recognition.

"Copper irises!" Abby stammered out. "Hallie's corsage is a copper iris, in her photo!"

"Right, and Ama wrote in her diary that they were her favorite flowers," I reminded them.

"It *cannot* be a coincidence," Camila declared.

"I know," I said. I turned to Sarah, who looked confused. "My mom said the mural was commissioned by Francis Coventry, right?"

"Well, yes and no," Sarah said. "At first, we thought the mural was painted when the house was built in the late 1880s. But as we restored it, we noticed the style of dresses the girls are wearing isn't from that period. So we did some digging. It turns out the mural was partially repainted in 1922, when the house became a school for girls.

"This room was a silent study room during that time," Sarah continued. "We think the figures of the girls in the mural were altered so they would represent students. See?" She pointed to a tiny gold fleur-de-lis, barely visible on the violin player's collar. "All the Coventry School girls wore these. The mural was plastered over when the school closed and the building was turned into a boardinghouse. This room became an office, and all the old stuff from the school and before was either sold or sent to the Missouri History Museum's archives."

I barely heard her. I was staring at the golden fleur-de-lis on the girl's collar. I studied the other

two girls in the mural—they were wearing identical fleur-de-lis pins. Something about the pins looked familiar.

"Hallie's wearing a pin like this in her photo!" I told Camila and Abby. As soon as the words came out of my mouth, an idea hit me like a bolt of lightning. In a flash, I knew how everything—Hallie, Ama, the copper irises, the compass, and the fleur-de-lis pins—could be connected. "Maybe Ama and Hallie went to the Coventry School together?" I blurted out.

Abby's eyes lit up. "Yes!" she said, practically shouting. "That has to be it!" She grinned at me. I smiled back, until I remembered I was still mad at her for saying I'd never find Hallie. I turned back and refocused on the mural. The girls in the painting smiled down at me looking calm, like they knew something I didn't.

"Is it okay if I take some photos?" I asked Sarah.

"Of course," she said, moving the ladder to a part of the wall that was still covered with plaster. I slipped my camera out of my backpack and switched it on. As Sarah picked up her plaster knife and brush,

The Mural in the Morning Room

I started taking photos. Her hands moved quickly, chipping off the cracked top layer of plaster. Abby and Camila stood next to her, looking up at the girls in the mural. The flakes of plaster fell down, swirling through the air like snow. From where I stood, it seemed like the girls in the mural were smiling right at Abby and Camila, as if they were all connected. Looking at them, I knew it would make a great photograph.

I raised my camera. Abby looked confused. "Are you taking a picture of us or the mural?" she asked.

"Um, sort of both. Just pretend I'm not here, okay?" I said. Abby looked curious, but then she gave me a little nod and went back to watching Sarah work.

Specks of plaster came loose as Sarah chipped at the wall, and the white dust floated toward Abby's and Camila's upturned faces. I set the camera on burst mode and started shooting as I moved around. Finally, I stopped and reviewed the shots. One of the shots was perfect—Abby and Camila smiled up at the mural, plaster snowflakes

on their shoulders, as the girls in the painting smiled down on them. I couldn't help smiling. For the first time in a long time, I'd taken exactly the picture I'd wanted to take.

It was almost time to go meet Dad, but Abby had to use a restroom. Sarah directed her to one down the back hall, where we'd seen Dodger on our last visit. "I'll be right back," said Abby, slipping through the side door.

Sarah put her earbuds back in and got back to work. I gave Camila a half smile, hoping she would say something, but she turned back to the mural and avoided my eyes. She was obviously still upset with me. Suddenly it felt like I was standing at the edge of an icy pool. Finally, I got the courage to dive in and say something. "Camila? I'm really sorry," I said. "You were right to get mad at me. I haven't been the best host."

It took a long moment, but finally Camila's eyes warmed a little. "I am sorry, too," she said. "I know you miss your grandmother, and you want to solve the mystery so you can feel close to her."

I blinked, surprised. I hadn't realized that

The Mural in the Morning Room

Ama was the reason I wanted to find Hallie, but once Camila said it, I knew she was right. "Yes," I admitted. "But I also want to be a good host. Tomorrow we should do what *you* want to do."

Camila let out a bright laugh. "Oh, Lea," she said, "I really *do* want to help find Hallie, you know."

"Really?" I said.

Camila nodded. "Of course I do, because you're my friend. *And* I want to try frozen custard," she replied. "And go see the Arch. And see Dodger. But we can do *all* of that, I think. Yes?"

"Yes," I said in a rush, and we hugged.

As we waited for Abby to come back, I thought about what I would say to her. I'd apologize for being too sensitive, I thought, but minutes passed, and there was no sign of Abby. It was weird.

"Perhaps she is still in the restroom," said Camila.

"Let's go check," I said. We went through the side door and made our way to the bathroom. When we opened the door, it was empty. Where had Abby gone? We were going to be late to meet Dad. "Maybe she got lost," I said. "We should look for her." Camila nodded.

We left the bathroom and moved quickly down the long hallway. I kept telling myself that Coventry House was big and it was easy to get lost, but I could feel worry tightening in my chest.

"Abby! *Abby!*" we called as we turned a corner. All I could hear was the creak of the floorboards as we moved. I was starting to get really worried. At the top of my lungs, I shouted—

"ABBY!" I held my breath, waiting for a response. Above us, I heard a faint noise.

"Abby?!" Camila called, looking up at the ceiling.

"Here, Dodger! Kitty, kitty, kitty? Dodger!" We could hear Abby's voice, one flight up.

Halfway back the way we'd come was a sagging set of side stairs. Camila and I raced to it and started up the steps, calling for Abby. We reached the second-floor landing. A pile of dusty old rope that looked like it was as old as the house was in the middle of the floor. We stepped over it as we moved ahead, still hearing Abby above us.

The stairs twisted up one more flight, but the steps were in bad shape. Some were splintered and cracked, and at the top, one was missing.

"Should we keep going?" Camila asked, frightened.

I knew Mom had told us that the upper levels of the house were still under major construction—but I also knew we needed to find Abby. If we could just get her to come downstairs, maybe none of us would get in trouble.

"Let's just go up one more floor slowly," I said. Camila gave a little worried nod. We edged up the stairs, gripping the side railing.

"Abby?" I called.

"Lea?! Is that you?" Abby sounded excited. "You guys have to come here!"

"Abby, we're not supposed to be up here! You need to be careful," I called, as I helped Camila up over the rotted step to the top of the third-floor landing.

My mom had said the upper floors of Coventry House were damaged, and when we stepped inside the first room off the landing, I gasped. In front of us there had once been a turret, but fire had burned away part of the circular room. On the far side, the thick brick wall had crumbled, revealing patches of

sky. The floorboards were singed and uneven, and in a few places, the wood was rotted through. Abby stood by a skeletal window frame, and a few feet away crouched the Artful Dodger.

Abby lit up when she saw us. "Look!" She pointed to the cat. "I've got him!"

Dodger did not look like he'd been "gotten" by anyone. His tail and most of his fur were sticking straight up, and his eyes were wide. When Abby reached for him, he backed up with a hiss, as if he was frightened. "It's okay," Abby murmured as she crept toward him. "I'm the cat whisperer, Dodger."

As Abby approached, Dodger watched silently, his tail twitching. As she reached down to pick him up, he leapt away.

"Dodger, no!" Abby squealed, lunging for him.

"Be careful!" I shouted, but Abby was already running after the kitten. As she crossed the floorboards, the wood groaned in a sickening, splintering sound.

Camila and I screamed, and I shut my eyes, terrified that Abby had fallen through the floor.

"Lea!!" Abby shrieked. "Help!"

I looked, and my stomach dropped. Abby was clinging to the window frame and standing on a narrow patch of floorboard, with Dodger at her feet. A giant hole gaped in front of them. One wrong move and Abby and Dodger would both fall in.

Trapped
Chapter 9

Abby stared at the hole in front of her, then up at me. Her eyes flashed with fear. "I'm going to fall!" she cried. Her voice sounded high and thin, like an alarm going off.

"Don't move!" I ordered, remembering when my dad was trapped on the cliff in Brazil. The rescuers had told him not to make any sudden movements, in case they triggered more rock or mud to collapse. "Hold on to the window frame. Stay still."

I turned to Camila, who looked just as scared as Abby. "Go down to the main floor and get help," I told her. Camila nodded and rushed back down the stairs.

"We're getting help, Abby," I called, trying to sound calm although my heart was racing. Even from across the room, I could see she was trembling.

 Trapped

She had wrapped her arms over the window ledge, gripping tightly.

"It's going to be okay," I reassured her, as Dodger cautiously approached and rubbed against her leg. "See? Dodger thinks so, too. He likes you. You *are* a cat whisperer."

Abby tried to smile, but her lower lip wobbled as she stared into the pit in front of her. "How far down do you think it is?" she said in a small voice.

"It doesn't matter, because you're not going to fall," I said, trying to sound confident.

Abby nodded as if she wanted to believe me. She shut her eyes. "I'm scared," she whispered.

"So am I," I told my best friend. "But you're going to be okay."

Abby shook her head. "You don't know that," she said, and her voice quavered. "What if the rest of this floor collapses, and I fall?"

She was right. The boards definitely looked as if they might not be able to support her weight for long. *There must be something I can do,* I thought. I remembered the coiled rope I'd seen on the second-floor landing.

"Hold on," I said. I could hear Abby trying not to cry as I raced out of the room and down to the landing below. The rope was so old that thick dust flew into my face like a puff of smoke when I picked it up. I coughed but kept moving, running back upstairs with the rope in my arms.

"Abby, here!" I called, coming back into the room. I threw her one end of the rope. "Put this through the loops on your jeans and tie it."

Abby carefully released the window frame so she could thread the rope around her waist twice. She knotted the end to her belt and locked her hands over the knot.

"What now?" she asked.

I looked around the turret room. Above me, a burned-out hole in the ceiling exposed a beam that hadn't been touched by fire. Seeing it made me remember a trick Abby and I had seen once when some movers delivered a piano to a house down the block. It was too big to go through the front door, so they used a pulley to haul it up to some big windows on the second floor and inside. I tossed my end of the rope over the rafter and ran with it over

Trapped

to the thick wooden post at the top of the stairs.

"Just in case something breaks," I said to Abby, "this will help." She nodded, watching as I wrapped my end of the rope around the thick wooden post, double-knotted my end to one of the loops, and tucked it under. *This will have to do*, I thought.

Just then, Abby screamed! I looked over my shoulder. Abby was still at the window, but Dodger was now on the sill beside her. "Sorry, false alarm," Abby said, releasing a nervous laugh. "He scared me."

Dodger purred, rubbing his head against Abby's hand on the window. When his tail flicked her cheek, she made a face.

"So *now* you want to be friends?" she said, but I could tell she was calming down. Abby reached over to pet the cat. As she shifted her weight, the boards under her cracked with a sound like fireworks exploding.

Abby yelped and hugged the window frame.

"Are you okay?" I asked.

She shook her head. "I don't want to just stand here until the rest of the floor gives out!"

111

Lea and Camila

I crouched down, studying the hole in the floor. It wasn't as big as it had seemed at first, but the broken boards were blackened and weakened by the fire. It was hard to know where on the floor you could step safely.

I lay on the ground and craned my neck, trying to see beneath the floor at the edge of the hole.

"What are you doing?" Abby said.

"Hold on," I replied. From this angle, I could see a support beam running under the floorboards where Abby stood. The beam was thick and sturdy-looking, and didn't appear to be blackened by fire.

Abby shifted her weight, and the floorboards groaned again. She clutched the rope around her waist and looked at me in panic.

"Step to your right and put one foot in front of the other," I told her.

She followed my instructions, putting her feet on top of where the beam was. "That feels more solid," she said.

"It is. There's a strong beam underneath. If you step straight ahead, you'll be on it the whole time, and you can walk over here."

Trapped

Abby looked at me—then down at the jagged hole in the floor beside her, terrified. "I can't," she said. This wasn't the fearless Abby I knew. A tear ran down her face.

"Yes, you can," I told her. "I'll help you." I grabbed the rope, leaving only enough slack for Abby to walk the few feet across to me. "The rope and the rafter will hold you up if you fall," I assured her.

Abby looked down at the hole again. In that moment, I tried to send her all the courage I had ever had.

Abby took a deep breath, then turned and grabbed Dodger, holding him under her arm. To my surprise, he didn't fight at all as she let go of the window frame and started across the room.

"Good," I said, sounding confident. I couldn't let her know I was scared. "Now walk straight."

Abby did as she was told, putting one foot in front of the other like a gymnast on a balance beam. Dodger mewed as they passed the edge of the pit, but Abby kept going across the rickety floor until she was nearly beside me. Then, with a deep sigh,

Lea and Camila

Abby took a giant step through the doorway onto the safety of the landing, and hugged me harder than she ever had before.

We were halfway down the stairs when we heard Camila and my parents calling our names from below. We met them on the second-floor landing. My mom looked surprised when she saw Abby holding Dodger, but she didn't say anything. She and Dad hugged us both, but I could tell they were really upset. I could see my father looking at the rope around Abby's waist, and I knew I'd have some explaining to do later.

As we tramped back downstairs, I started to confess what had happened, but Abby interrupted me.

"Mr. and Mrs. Clark, it was all my fault. I saw Dodger and I forgot about everything else," she said as we reached the front entry hall. "Camila and Lea were just trying to help, and Lea saved me!"

I felt a surge of pride.

"That's sweet of you to say, Abby," Mom replied sternly, "but none of you should have gone upstairs. You could have been seriously hurt!"

 Trapped

I felt my pride crumble, replaced by shame. I studied my feet, not wanting to see the disappointment in my mother's eyes.

"Not to mention," she continued, "that if anyone had been injured, the city could have shut down the entire restoration of Coventry House."

"Well, now, that didn't happen," Dad said soothingly. "The girls are safe, and as an added bonus, they have a cat!"

"Thank goodness no one was hurt," Mom said. I could hear the anxiety in her voice. She rubbed her forehead.

Camila, Abby, and I shared a guilty look. I was glad we'd saved Dodger, but I hated letting my mother down. "I'm really sorry," I said.

Mom softened a bit. "I know you are. I hope I can trust that you will never do it again."

We all nodded. Dodger squirmed in Abby's arms. I scratched him under his chin and he started purring, rubbing his head over my hand. "We still need to help Dodger," I said in a small voice.

"Yes," Camila chimed in. "What will happen to him?"

Lea and Camila

"My mom should take a look at him," said Abby. She turned to me. "He can stay at our house, since I know your dad is allergic."

"That sounds like a plan," Dad said. "Let's get going before Dodger changes his mind."

***

On the way home, I asked Dad if we could stop for frozen custard. "Camila wants to try it before she goes back," I said. Camila beamed at me.

At Ted Drewes, we got concretes—custard with the toppings mixed in. Camila and I got our custard with pralines and caramel sauce, while Abby got hers with fresh cherries and hot fudge. Camila ate hers so fast she got a melted custard mustache—and a brain freeze! "Mmmmmm," she kept saying between bites, as Dad drove us home.

Dodger was curled on the backseat between me and Abby, napping comfortably. He didn't seem to miss Coventry House too much.

Dad drove to Abby's house, a few blocks from ours. Abby's mom examined Dodger, checking his eyes, ears, teeth, and fur.

Trapped

"He's thin," she noted, "but he looks generally healthy. Abby and I will clean and de-flea him. And Lea, if you take a nice picture of him, we can make a flyer."

"Yes!" enthused Abby. "We'll hang it in the veterinary office. Customers are sometimes looking for cats or dogs to adopt." She gave me a shy smile, and I smiled back.

When it was time for us to head home, Abby walked us out. As Dad and Camila continued down the front steps, Abby took my arm.

"Hey," she said, stopping. She seemed nervous, very un-Abby-like. "Thanks again for saving me."

"I didn't really save you, Abby," I pointed out. After all, it's not like I had airlifted her out of there, the way Dad was rescued by the helicopter in Brazil. "You saved yourself," I added.

"Well, I couldn't have saved *myself* without you," Abby argued, sounding more like herself. Still, her chin wobbled a little, and her eyes looked wet. "I'm *really* sorry for saying you might not find Hallie," she said. "And I'm even sorrier for making you cry."

Lea and Camila

"I know," I said, trying not to cry again. Only this time it wasn't from anger. "I'm sorry too. I overreacted."

"I don't want you to be mad at me." Abby wiped her eyes. "Lea, you're my best friend."

"You're my best friend, too," I said in a rush, relieved. "I'm sorry about getting so upset before. At first I really liked that you and Camila got along so well. But after a while, I started to feel bad about it. I felt like maybe you guys preferred hanging out without me."

Abby looked stunned. "Are you *kidding*?" she said. "This whole time I was trying to be extra-nice and friendly to Camila, because she was your special friend and I wanted to make you happy." She looked down and added, "Also, I was worried that you liked her more than me."

"Really?" I said in disbelief.

Abby gave a hard little nod. "Ever since you got back from Brazil, all you've talked about is how great Camila is, and then how she was coming to visit. I thought maybe when she got here that you would forget all about me and just want to hang out with

her," she confessed. "Then of course I met her, and she was really fun, but I was still sort of worried."

"Oh, Abby, you're crazy," I said through a smile. "You'll always be my best friend."

"I know that *now*!" Abby snorted, and then giggled. She slung an arm around my shoulders. "Lea, you'll always be my best friend, too."

After dinner, I pulled out the photograph of Hallie again, and Camila and I stared at it.

"I don't see anything new," I said with a sigh.

Camila looked thoughtful. "Perhaps we should do as Ms. Garcia says and look at things in a new way."

"Okay, but how?" I threw myself onto my bed, frustrated. My eyes came to rest on the photo on my bedside table—the one of Ama with the Masai warrior in Africa. Ama was sunburned under her bush hat and she looked tired, but her compass still hung around her neck, and she wore a triumphant smile. I remembered her telling me once that on the way to Mount Kilimanjaro, she and her guide had

Lea and Camila

come to a river where the bridge had been washed away by rain. "I was worried we wouldn't make it," she had said, "but the guide led us downstream to another place where we could cross. There's always more than one way to get where you want to go."

Suddenly, I felt a burst of inspiration. "Hold on!" I said, sitting up. "We've just been searching for information about *Hallie*. But maybe instead we should look for more information about *Ama*. That would be easier to find, and it could lead us to Hallie if she and Ama are connected."

"That's true," Camila agreed enthusiastically. "But where?"

Yes, *where*? I'd already reread Ama's journals, and I hadn't found anything about Hallie there. Where else could I look? Then I remembered.

The attic. After Ama had passed away, Mom had given away many of her clothes and books, but she'd kept a box or two of Ama's mementos and stored them in our attic. Maybe if Camila and I looked through them, we'd find something that could help us solve the mystery and uncover the connection between Ama, Hallie, and the compass necklace.

A Bridge to the Past
Chapter 10

Dad was surprised when I asked him if Camila and I could search the attic, but he didn't say no. He came upstairs to the hall outside my room and pulled the attic ladder down from the ceiling.

Camila looked up nervously at the narrow wooden stepladder to the attic. I could tell she was thinking about Abby getting stranded upstairs at Coventry House.

"Don't worry," I assured her. "It's totally safe."

Camila gave a sharp nod. She gritted her teeth and followed me up as Dad watched us.

In a corner of the attic we found the boxes marked "Ama" and began digging through them. They were packed with loose photos and souvenirs from all over the world: masks from Mexico, a kimono from Japan, a wooden flute from Peru.

I sifted through photos of Ama on the Great Wall of China and swimming in New Zealand.

We kept searching. Camila pulled out an old, dusty photo sleeve from inside an overstuffed book. When she opened it, her eyes widened. "*Look*," she said, handing it to me.

Inside was a black-and-white photo of a young Ama in a pleated skirt and a dark jacket. Pinned to the lapel was a metal pin—a fleur-de-lis.

"Look, look! She went to the Coventry School, like Hallie!" I blurted.

"You were right!" Camila said, wide-eyed.

An electric thrill zipped through me. I turned to Camila. "You wanted to help me find Hallie, and you did! This photo could help lead us to her!" Camila and I beamed at each other. I looked at Ama's picture again and knew there was someone else who'd want to see this.

When Camila and I came down from the attic, I told her I'd be right back. Clutching Ama's photo, I raced downstairs, heading for Mom's office off the dining room. But as soon as I turned into the front hall, I heard her voice coming from the kitchen.

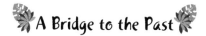

"This is a disaster," she said, sounding upset.

"Maybe you can talk to them," I heard Dad say.

"I *did*," Mom said. "They said they've made their decision."

I stayed in the hallway shadows, unsure what to do. When I looked out, I could see my parents standing in the kitchen.

Dad put a comforting hand on Mom's arm. "Hey," he said. "Don't give up. Maybe the Preservation Society can find another sponsor."

"It's almost *all* our funding," Mom said quietly. "If we don't get another sponsor for the restoration soon, it'll be too late. The bank will foreclose on it and sell it off to developers. Coventry House will be torn down."

The next day was chilly enough to make me shiver as I looked out the van window while we headed downtown. The gray sky threatened to darken into storm clouds any minute. It looked the way I felt right now—sad and hazy. I couldn't stop thinking about Coventry House being torn down.

Lea and Camila

Soon our destination came into view—the silver loop of the Gateway Arch. Next to me, Camila stretched her neck for a better look. As we got closer, the Arch loomed over us, huge. You can take a tram to the top, and the city views are unforgettable. Although Camila had wanted to visit the Arch, with her fear of heights I didn't know if she would want to go all the way up.

The van dropped us off near the Arch. As we walked toward it, Ms. Garcia told us, "It's called the Gateway Arch because St. Louis was regarded as America's Gateway to the West. In the 19th century, pioneers had to cross the Mississippi River and pass through St. Louis before they went west. So in a way, the Arch celebrates how the city was like a bridge from America's past to its future."

By now, we were much closer. The Arch stretched over us like a steel rainbow. "This is the most photographed place in St. Louis," Ms. Garcia said as we all looked up. "Your challenge is going to be to find fresh ways to shoot it. I know you can do it! Is everyone ready to go up and start taking photos?"

I glanced at Camila. She was staring up at the

Arch, looking anxious. "Don't worry," I said, squeezing her arm. "We'll be with you the whole time."

We crowded inside the sleek silver tram. After a long moment, it started moving, lifting straight up from underneath. It felt like we were inside a spaceship taking off.

"Whoa," said Abby.

Camila sucked in her breath. I knew she was afraid. It didn't help that Kevin kept repeating, "We're going so high! We're going so high!"

Camila put her hand on the wall, flat, like she was trying to stay standing. "Just breathe. You're doing a great job!" I whispered. She gasped as the tram turned, curving up the spine of the Arch, and then slowed to a stop as we reached the top.

"We're now at the highest point in the city," said Ms. Garcia, as we exited onto the observation deck. "Six hundred and thirty feet above the ground."

The buildings, parks, and streets lay below in a complicated puzzle. From here, City Hall looked like a matchbox with a dome. I wanted to show Camila, but her eyes were closed again.

"Camila, you have to see this—it's incredible!"

I said. "You know, sometimes the best experiences are also the hardest. Remember in Brazil, how afraid I was to snorkel? But I'm so glad I did it."

Slowly, Camila opened her eyes. As she did, the sun started to come out, making the city below glitter. "Wow," Camila said softly, her eyes full of wonder.

"Look—City Museum!" I said, pointing out the jumble of colored pipes with the yellow bus on its roof in the distance. Camila took it in, fascinated. I could tell she was forgetting her fear, because she lifted up her camera and looked through it. I took out my camera too and circled the observation deck, looking out the windows at the city. I noticed how the sunlight reflected off the shimmering Mississippi, and how Eads Bridge looked like an iron spiderweb, and the intricate patchwork of parks, buildings, and streets that stretched to the horizon. It was like I was seeing St. Louis for the first time.

Soon, we stepped back on the tram. As it accelerated down, Camila yelped, but she looked excited, not scared. By the time we reached the ground and the tram's doors opened, she was giggling. Camila turned to me. "It is as you said, Lea. You cannot let your fear stop you."

After the trip up inside the Arch, I felt inspired. Ms. Garcia gave us twenty minutes to take photos, and everywhere I turned, I had a new idea. I took pictures from the base of the Arch looking straight up, and a bunch more running toward it. The time flew by, and suddenly it was time to leave. I had been too busy trying to capture what I was seeing and how I was feeling to notice.

"How did it go?" Ms. Garcia asked us as the class walked back to the van.

"Good," said Camila. "I took one I like—look!" She held out her camera for us to see. It was a photograph of me, running in front of the Arch. My hair was blowing around, and I was jumping, caught in midair, trying to get my shot with my camera. I looked really happy.

"Wow," said Ms. Garcia. "*That* is a great action shot, Camila!"

Camila looked pleased. "Thank you," she

replied. "I think Lea looks very like her grandmother Ama in this."

"Lea, you do!" Abby echoed. Camila showed me the photo again. They were right. My head was tilted back, and my hair caught the light as it bounced behind me. I looked bold and free, just like Ama did in the photo of her jumping over that rock on Bondi Beach.

"What about you, Lea?" asked Ms. Garcia as we reached the van. "May I see some of the pictures you took?" I nodded, handing her my camera. "Very nice," she said, scrolling through the shots I'd taken while I was running. She scrolled back even further. When she came to the shot of Abby and Camila in front of the girls in the Coventry House mural, she paused. For a moment I thought something was wrong, but when Ms. Garcia looked at me she seemed really impressed.

"Lea," she said, "this photo is truly striking. The composition makes it seem as if the girls in the painting are looking at Abby and Camila."

I nodded. "That was the idea," I said, pleased she'd noticed.

"You've really found your eye," she said. "This is exceptional."

I was so happy, I felt like doing cartwheels. Ms. Garcia liked my photo!

"The mural in the picture is striking, too," she continued. "Where is it?"

"In Coventry House, in Old North St. Louis," I replied. *But it might not be there for long*, I thought sadly, as she handed me back my camera.

At lunch, I told Camila and Abby about Coventry House possibly being torn down. *"What?"* said Abby, taking a bite of her peanut butter and banana sandwich. "After all the work they're doing on it? Why?"

"My mom said it would happen if they don't get the funding they need," I replied. I scrunched up my sandwich wrapper and threw it in the trash. "When I think about that, finding Hallie doesn't seem so important anymore."

Abby frowned. "Lea, what are you talking about? I know how much you want to find Hallie.

If you don't find out the whole story, you'll always have questions."

I nodded, but I still felt worried. "I guess I'm just afraid," I admitted. "What if, even after I search, I never discover anything more about Hallie?"

"You must not let your fears stop you," Camila said. "It is as you said in the Arch: When something is difficult, that is when you must continue."

Camila was right, and I knew Ama wouldn't want me to quit, either. She'd want me to keep moving forward to find Hallie. And I thought I knew where we needed to go.

The Coventry School for Girls

Chapter 11

When Dad picked us up, I asked if he could take us to the Missouri History Museum's Library and Research Center. Sarah the art restorer had said that when the Coventry School closed, all its papers had been taken there, so that seemed like the best place to look next.

My dad was pleased at my sudden interest in the History Museum's library. "It's a pretty fantastic place," he said as we drove toward Forest Park.

My father was right. The research center was across from Forest Park, in a domed yellow brick building that Dad said had once been a Jewish temple. He dropped us off and promised to meet us in an hour.

"Do you know where we're going?" Camila asked as we headed inside.

"I think so," I said, even though I wasn't totally sure. In the lobby, Abby and Camila followed me across the polished stone floor to a wall map, which said that the Archives and Photographs Department was ahead on the left.

We moved through a double-doored entrance into a gigantic reading room. Above us soared the huge, stained-glass dome. It was so quiet I could hear Abby suck in her breath as we walked down the aisle, past people reading.

"I sure hope you know what you're doing," she whispered to me.

A few adults looked up as I led Abby and Camila up to the main information desk. A tall librarian sat there, looking at his computer screen.

I cleared my throat. "Hello," I said.

Seeing me, the librarian blinked hard and turned up the corners of his mouth in the tiniest smile I'd ever seen. "May I help you?" he asked.

"Yes," I said, trying to sound confident. "I need to look at the enrollment records for the Coventry School for Girls between 1952 and 1956, please."

The librarian managed to raise his eyebrows and

narrow his eyes at the same time. "How old are you?" he asked.

"Um, ten?" I told him, feeling self-conscious.

"Do you have a parent with you?"

I shook my head.

"Well then, my apologies, but our policy is that children under sixteen need an adult to do research. I think it best that you come back with a responsible grown-up." Before any of us could reply, he walked off, leaving us standing there.

Camila looked confused. "What is going on?" she asked.

"He won't help us because we're kids," said Abby, upset. "What are we supposed to do? We can't just leave—"

"We're not leaving," I told her. I was angry at myself. I should have asked Dad to stay, or called ahead about the archive's policies. My father had given me his cell phone in case of an emergency, but I was guessing my parents wouldn't think this qualified as one. Still, it felt like one to me. By the time Dad returned to pick us up, the archive would be closed, and who knew when I'd be able to come

back. Time was running out. I needed to fix this problem myself.

"Wait here," I said, and marched after the librarian. He was about to go through a door marked "Restricted" when I stepped in front of him.

"Excuse me," he said. "This is a restricted area!"

"I'm sorry, sir," I said, my voice firm. A few of the adults working at tables looked over. "May I please speak with you?" I asked.

The librarian gave the adults a weak little smile. It evaporated as soon as he looked at me. He folded his arms. "I'm busy. What is it?" he asked in a low voice.

I launched in, explaining as fast as I could about finding Hallie's photo, and Ama and Coventry House. As I talked, Abby and Camila joined us. I told the librarian how the hunt had led us to the Jewel Box, the main library, and now here. "I may not be an adult, but that doesn't mean I'm not doing real research. I *am*," I finished passionately.

"Interesting," said the librarian. After a long moment, he spoke again. "So you're looking for records from the Coventry School for Girls?"

Abby, Camila, and I nodded eagerly.

The librarian let go of a sigh so big he seemed to deflate. "We house the school's complete academic and registration records here," he told us. "*You* can't look at them, of course . . . but I suppose there's no harm if you watch *me* look at them." Then, out of nowhere, he winked at us.

We sat at a long table and waited until the librarian returned with the Coventry School registry from 1952. "What name am I looking for?" he asked, opening the wide leather book.

"Amanda Silva," I said, remembering Ama's last name before she married Grandpa Bill.

The librarian flipped through the pale green pages. After a minute or two, he stopped. "There!" he said, looking pleased with himself. At the top of the page was a small black-and-white school photo of Ama as a girl, smiling brightly.

"Amanda Silva, eighth grade," read Abby over the librarian's shoulder. "It has her address here and everything!"

Pride soared through me. I'd been right! Ama *had* been a student at Coventry!

The librarian scanned the page and said, "It says here she withdrew at the end of the school year."

"What does it mean, 'withdrew'?" Camila asked.

"It means she left," replied the librarian.

"Because they moved to West County!" I chimed in, recalling what Mom had told me. Thinking about Ama having to leave her school and friends made me sad for her. I couldn't imagine having to move away from Lafayette Square and Abby. The more I thought about it, the more certain I felt that Hallie and Ama had been friends at the Coventry School. But I didn't yet have any proof.

"There should be a girl named Hallie in the same grade," I said to the librarian.

He read off names as he turned the pages. "Mary, Shirley, Deborah, Lynn . . . " Finally he reached the last page. "There's no Hallie, I'm sorry."

No Hallie? That couldn't be right! Disappointment flooded through me. *They had to have gone to school together*, I thought, feeling a sharp pang squeeze my heart. I was so close to figuring it

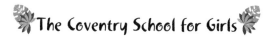

out. What was I missing?

"Maybe Hallie is a nickname?" Abby piped up.

"You're right!" I said, excitement lifting me up. "Her real name could be something else. Maybe we can recognize her photograph!"

As the librarian turned back to the start of the eighth-grade section, I pulled out my photo of Hallie at the Jewel Box. She would have been a little older in this picture than in her school photo, but I still hoped it would help us recognize Hallie if we saw her.

Carefully, the librarian flipped through the pages of eighth-grade girls. We studied each little black-and-white picture. Some girls had horn-rimmed glasses, others wore bows in their hair, but none of them looked like Hallie.

The librarian turned a page, and suddenly I squinted at one of the photos. The girl's hair was longer, and her face rounder, but her eyes met the camera in the bold gaze I had come to know so well.

"Hallie!" I said, too loud.

The librarian shushed me, but his eyes had

sparks in them. "That's her?" he asked, showing Abby and Camila, too. We compared the two photos and agreed it was definitely Hallie.

"Harriet Emmeline Leland," I read. "There's even an address."

"It may well be out of date," the librarian said. "However, we have access here to the public city records. If you like, I can do a search under her name."

I nodded, still in disbelief. A few days ago when I'd found Hallie's photo, she'd seemed so far away. It was thrilling to think there was a chance that she could still be right here in St. Louis.

Twenty minutes later, we met my dad outside. We all started telling him what had happened—at the same time. "Hold on!" he laughed. "Pick a spokesperson, please."

"We found Hallie!" I said. "Her name's Harriet Leland—and that's not all. We have an address for her! Well, we have an address for a Harriet Leland Dumond," I said, handing him the slip of paper where I'd written it down.

Dad looked at it, impressed. "It's in the Central West End," he said. "That's close to here."

"Can we go see if it's her?" I begged. "Please?!"

Dad grinned. "Why not? Maybe Hallie will be at home."

I'd been to the Central West End before, but as we drove through the neighborhood, the homes looked bigger than I remembered. Mansions with marble columns sat on wide rolling lawns. Some had wrought-iron gates that looked as if only a giant could move them, while other houses hid behind enormous pine trees. Our old Victorian on Hickory Street seemed like a playhouse by comparison.

"Here it is, 453 Lenox Street," Dad said, as we pulled up to a gray stone mansion with long windows.

A cobblestone path wound past a pair of granite lion statues up to a dark blue door. *Is this really Hallie's house?* I wondered. I might be about to meet a long-lost friend of my grandmother's!

Lea and Camila

Nervous butterflies started fluttering in my stomach.

Before I could say anything, Abby threw open the car door. "Come on!" she said. "We have to see if she's home!"

I held my breath as we raced up to the front door.

"Lea, you knock," said Camila.

I took a breath, trying to calm the butterflies. I was a little scared, but more than that, I felt excited. I knocked on the door. After a long moment, the old-fashioned brass peephole opened. A blue eye squinted out at us.

"Yes?" said a man's voice.

"Hello," I said. "We're looking for Hallie? I mean, Harriet Leland Dumond?"

The door opened abruptly. A middle-aged man in an expensive-looking suit stood before us. "May I help you?" he asked, frowning.

"I hope so," Dad said. "I'm Mike Clark," he said, offering his hand. The man didn't shake it.

"Justus Dumond," he said instead, as if we should know that already.

"Right!" said my dad. "Good! Yes! Now, let's see, Mr. Dumont—"

"Du*mond*," the man corrected him.

"Dumond, yes," Dad stammered. "My daughter Lea has a theory—mind you, a theory based on actual research—that my late mother-in-law *knew* Mrs. Dumond—"

"Hallie," I interrupted. "They were classmates at the Coventry School."

While we talked, Justus Dumond crossed his arms, taking in Dad's baggy shorts, worn loafers, and the black socks he wore pulled halfway up his shins. Finally he broke in.

"Harriet is my mother, and she's quite frail. It wouldn't be suitable to bother her with this right now."

"But we wouldn't really be *bothering* her—" Abby started to say.

"Yes, you would," Justus replied sharply. And before anyone could say anything else, he stepped back—and shut the door in our faces!

We stood there, shocked. My dad let out a little surprised laugh, but stopped when he saw my face.

I felt like a balloon that had suddenly popped. All the hope and excitement flooded out of me. Abby put a hand on my shoulder as I took a ragged breath, feeling tears rise. I knew Ama wouldn't want me to cry. But I didn't know what else to do.

Hallie

Chapter 12

I couldn't quite believe it. It didn't seem possible that even though I'd tracked Hallie down, I wasn't going to get a chance to talk to her. Abby and Camila each put a comforting arm around me.

"Well," said Dad sadly, "I guess that's that."

No, it's not, I thought to myself, feeling my temper rise. Impulsively, I reached up and knocked on the door, hard. Dad, Camila, and Abby looked worried, but I kept my eyes glued to the brass peephole. After a moment, it clicked open and Justus Dumond's eye appeared. Summoning my best manners, I plunged ahead.

"I am so sorry, Mr. Dumond," I said to the peephole. "We didn't mean to disturb you and your mother. Can you please let her know that Amanda Silva's granddaughter is here?"

Behind the door, Justus coughed, annoyed.

"Please?" I said, pleading. "If she doesn't want to see me, we'll go away and never bother you again."

"Fine," Justus muttered through the door after a moment. The peephole clicked shut.

"Great save, Lea!" Dad said.

I allowed myself to resume breathing. We stood there for what felt like an hour. Right as I was beginning to think that maybe Justus wasn't coming back, the door opened abruptly to reveal him in the doorway, red-faced and awkward.

"Right this way," he said, and just like that, he let us in.

We followed Justus down a hallway lined with oil paintings. He pushed open a dark wooden door and we entered a large room with a Persian rug. Antique maps of different sizes and colors crowded the walls from floor to ceiling. There was a map of Africa as tall as a grandfather clock, and framed photos of strange, beautiful buildings and landscapes I didn't recognize. Even though the room was unfamiliar, oddly enough I felt right at home.

"Wow," Dad said, glancing around.

A rustling noise made me turn. Across the room, a pair of glass doors opened onto a sunny garden. Sitting just outside at a tiny wicker patio table was a white-haired woman. I knew it was Hallie because when she looked at me, her eyes and mouth curved in the same warm, secret way as they had in her photo. She was wearing a silky navy dress and cardigan. As she rose to greet us, I saw the compass necklace hanging around her neck.

My heart began to pound. I felt Camila's hand slip into mine, and I gave it a grateful squeeze.

"Hello," said Hallie, her gaze drifting from Dad to Abby to Camila to me. "Which one of you is Amanda Silva's granddaughter?" Her eyes caught mine, and she smiled. "I'm guessing it's you," she said. "You look very like Amanda."

I nodded, suddenly feeling tongue-tied. I'd been so focused on *finding* Hallie, I hadn't really ever thought about what I would say if we finally met.

Luckily, Abby didn't have that problem. "I can't believe we found you!" she said in a rush.

"Yes," said Hallie gently, as Justus helped her over to a leather chair. "How *did* you find me?" I

145

pulled out the photograph of her as a girl from my backpack and showed her.

"I found this at Coventry House," I said, and launched into the whole story of how we'd managed to figure out who she was. By the time I was done, even Justus seemed impressed.

"Were you and my grandmother friends at the Coventry School?" I asked Hallie.

"Not just friends," Hallie replied. "We were *kindred spirits*. I was so lucky to find her. She was the only person I liked at that horrid school."

"Horrid?" I said, surprised.

Hallie laughed. "Well, that's how I thought of it at the time. I hated that they made us wear uniforms and expected us to act like ladies all the time. We had to learn how to pour tea, fold napkins, waltz, and cross our legs in the proper way," she said, shaking her head. "I found it all intensely boring. But once I met Amanda, things got better. Your grandmother was never boring!"

Hallie described how she had met Ama in eighth-grade geography class. "She knew the names of every capital city in Africa, and she was *interested*

in them. She kept a list of all the places she wanted to visit. I started doing that, too. Amanda was more talkative and daring than I was, but we both shared a desire for travel and adventure."

"Where did you want to go?" asked Camila.

"Everywhere!" Hallie's face lit up. "I wanted to leave and never come home, to live abroad forever. Amanda's goal was to travel to every country in the world. Naturally, neither of our families approved."

"Why not?" asked Abby.

"Oh, many reasons," said Hallie. "My family had been part of St. Louis society for a hundred years. They thought I should become a debutante, then get married and have children. They had my life all planned out for me, before it had even begun!" She laughed, but I could see sadness in her eyes. "Amanda's father just didn't understand her. His family had worked hard to come from Brazil to America when he was a youngster, so he couldn't see why she would ever want to leave, even just to travel."

"But *you* understood," I said.

Hallie smiled her small, secret smile again, and

nodded. "The year we were in school together, we talked about where we would go, and the adventures we would have." She touched the compass around her neck, as if she was remembering.

"Where did you get that compass necklace?" I asked.

"One day, at a shop downtown, we found a pair of matching compasses," she said. "We decided we would make them into necklaces and wear them forever. That way we would never forget our friendship and dreams. And when we first put them on, we promised to each other that no matter what happened, someday we would travel and explore." Hallie gazed into the distance for a moment, the corners of her eyes crinkling at the memory.

"After Amanda moved away and the school closed, we lost touch. Still, I always remembered the promise we made—and I always wore this compass. It reminded me of what I really wanted—and gave me the strength to fulfill my dreams." She looked up at me. "I hope your grandmother was able to do the same," she said wistfully.

"She was," I replied. I told Hallie a little about

Ama's adventures—and that no matter where she went, Ama always wore her compass necklace. Hallie smiled.

"Do you still have it?" she asked.

"No," I said. When I told Hallie about how I gave the necklace away in Brazil to Yemanjá, the Goddess of the Sea, her eyes glistened.

"That sounds exactly like something Amanda would do," she said, and put her hand lightly on mine.

"What about *you*?" Camila asked Hallie. "Did you have adventures?"

"Oh, *yes*," Hallie said, and her face warmed with the memory. "After high school, I took the federal civil service exam and went to work for the U. S. State Department. I lived all over the world: Paris, Indonesia, Australia, Madagascar, and a few more places," she said proudly. "Every time I moved to a new country I used to think to myself, maybe I'll run into Amanda somewhere—in a cafe in Montmartre or perhaps on a beach in Sydney."

"I had no idea your friendship was so special," said Justus to Hallie. It sounded almost as if he was apologizing.

"It was," said Hallie. "She inspired me—and I bet I'm not the only one she inspired. After all, Lea, you wanted to find me just because I was wearing Amanda's compass necklace!" She squeezed my hand and I squeezed hers back, feeling a flood of affection.

Hallie's eyes drifted to the old photo of herself. "Goodness, I was so young," she said, sounding almost surprised.

"How old were you?" I asked.

"Sixteen," Hallie replied. "It was my coming-out party as a debutante. My parents threw a big party at the Jewel Box to celebrate. I didn't want one, of course. It seemed so old-fashioned and against everything that I believed in, but my mother insisted. Amanda wasn't going to come, but I told her I could only stand it if she was there. So she borrowed one of my fancy dresses and she came."

Hallie's face clouded.

"That was the last time I saw her," she said. "The Coventry School closed a few months later, and my parents sent me off to boarding school in Chicago." She gazed at a vase of flowers on the mantel.

Looking at the vase, I recognized the flowers.

"Copper irises!" I exclaimed. I pointed at the photo in Hallie's hands. "You're wearing a copper iris corsage here, and Ama mentioned them in her diary. She said they reminded her of your promise."

Hallie's face bloomed into a smile. "Yes. Amanda and I loved copper irises."

"They're on the mural at Coventry House, too!" said Camila.

"That's right, I had forgotten that mural," Hallie exclaimed. "I think that's why we liked them so much. Also, the fleur-de-lis is patterned after the iris, so it reminded us of our friendship. In the language of flowers, you know, the iris symbolizes friendship."

"Plus, you use the iris in your eye to *see*," Abby chimed in, "and both of you wanted to *see* the world."

"True," Hallie said, chuckling, "although I don't think we quite made *that* connection." She smiled, and as she looked from Abby to Camila to me, she looked so happy, she almost seemed to glow. "Thank you girls for finding me," Hallie said. "I'm so glad to know that Amanda fulfilled her dreams, just as I

did." Hallie sat back in her chair and sighed. She seemed tired all of a sudden.

I realized it had grown late. The sunset's light was filling the room. Dad cleared his throat and said we should get going, but as I picked up my backpack, an idea struck me. "May I take your picture?" I asked.

Hallie nodded, pleased. I pulled out my camera from my backpack and showed Hallie where to stand, in front of the glass door so that she was backlit by the golden light of the setting sun. She didn't even seem to mind when I adjusted her position a little.

"Lea," said Dad, "we don't want to take up all of Hallie's time."

"It's fine," Hallie said gently as I turned her another smidge. "I can tell that Lea is an artist."

I switched on my flash, then stepped back and found Hallie in the viewfinder. The angle, the light, the compass necklace, and her expression . . . it was all exactly right.

I held my breath and took the picture.

Picture Perfect

Chapter 13

On the last day of camp, I got up early to check my e-mail. The night before, I'd written to Zac and told him all about finding Hallie. I'd even e-mailed him the photo I'd taken of her, along with a scan of the original photo. I was betting he would think the whole story was pretty incredible, but when I checked my inbox, I had no new messages.

I tried not to let it get me down. Zac was really busy working at the animal sanctuary in Brazil. I knew he felt personally responsible for protecting the animals in the area, so I figured he was spending most of his time in the rainforest and probably just wasn't going online much.

I was worried about Zac, but I tried to put it out of my mind as we drove to camp. The class was spending all day in the photo studio at COCA,

printing and framing our two favorite photos to
show at the end-of-camp exhibit that night. First,
Ms. Garcia helped us all crop and adjust the color
and saturation of our photos so they looked exactly
the way we wanted. Then she printed the shots we'd
chosen on the giant photo printer in the corner. The
images were different sizes, but each one was printed
on satin-smooth photography paper and laid out on
a long table to dry.

"Wow. This looks amazing!" said Abby, staring
at her photograph of the Clydesdale horses at Soulard
Market. She was right: The horses looked as if they
were going to jump off the paper at any moment,
snorting and tossing their manes.

"Abby, we'll start with your photo," said
Ms. Garcia. She selected a cream-colored mat board.
As everyone gathered around, Ms. Garcia put the
board facedown on a mat cutter. She set the razor-
sharp cutting tool to the right width and length and
sliced out an exact square from the middle in a few
quick strokes. She handed the finished mat frame
to Abby, who fit the opening over her photo of the
horses. It looked perfect.

Picture Perfect

One by one, Ms. Garcia cut different-colored mats for everyone's pictures. My photo of Camila and Abby looking at the Coventry House mural got a pale lavender mat frame. Camila's picture of me in front of the Arch got one in dove gray.

While Ms. Garcia supervised, we centered the photos in their mat frames and then secured them with tiny pieces of double-sided mounting tape. As I worked, Abby peeked over my shoulder. Now that the photo was blown up, you could see every detail. Camila and Abby tilted their faces up to the girls in the mural, as flakes of plaster swirled around them.

"Wow," said Abby, in wonder. "I can't believe I'm a part of such a beautiful picture." My cheeks turned pink with pride.

The second photo I had selected to display was my portrait of Hallie wearing her compass necklace. When I'd shown it to Ms. Garcia, she'd suggested that we put the original photograph of Hallie from 1956 beside it. She even cut me a double mat for both pictures! When I lined up the mat frame over the portraits of Hallie, you could really see the similarities. Hallie at seventy-six stood the same way

she did at sixteen, with her hands clasped at the waist. In both pictures her lips curved in the same warm, secret smile. She was beautiful at any age.

As my eyes moved from the older portrait to the one I'd taken, I felt a surge of pride that I'd been able to capture Hallie's expression exactly the way I'd hoped.

"How's it going?" Ms. Garcia asked, coming up to me.

I shrugged. "Okay, I think."

Ms. Garcia looked over my prints with a sharp eye, and then gave an approving smile. "You've really grown this week, Lea—both your skills and your eye. Your work is beautiful. I'd like to submit both of your photos to be published in the COCA magazine, if that's all right with you."

I felt dazed. Behind her, Camila and Abby were nodding and giving me two silent thumbs-up.

"And Lea," Ms. Garcia said, her eyes meeting mine, "you should consider photography as a career."

"Thank you," I said. My voice was quiet, but inside, my heart was singing. There had been so many times this week when I'd felt sure that I had no idea what I was doing, so knowing that

 Picture Perfect

Ms. Garcia thought my work was good made me feel wonderful. The most important thing, though, was the fact that I loved both photos. As I thought about that, I realized that when Ms. Garcia had told us we needed to learn to "see in a new way," she'd really just meant we needed the confidence to see for ourselves.

Ms. Garcia moved over to Camila's pictures. "This one turned out so well," she said, looking at a shot of the Great Room at Coventry House. Camila had really captured the room's elegance, and the buzz of all the people working to restore it. Looking at it made me feel like I was standing right there.

"Is this the same house as the one with the mural?" Ms. Garcia asked. We nodded. As I looked at the photo of the Great Room again, sadness rose in me. Unless something changed soon, I thought, photographs would be the only way anyone would ever be able to see Coventry House.

That night, my parents, Camila, and I arrived at COCA for the exhibit. Sparkly lights were strung

over the front entrance to the trees around it, creating a starry, swooping canopy to walk under. Inside, the sculpture class had constructed papier-mâché mobiles that hung from the lobby ceiling, while easels scattered everywhere displayed watercolors and oil paintings done by the advanced art students. Our photographs hung in neat rows on the walls throughout the crowded space.

I spotted Abby and her mom in front of Abby's photos. "Have you seen Abby's masterpiece?" her mom asked, gesturing to the picture of the Clydesdale horses. She gave Abby a hug. "I had no *idea* you were such a talented photographer, honey! I should hire you to take some pet photos for my office."

"Really?" Abby squeaked. She looked at me, eyes dancing. "Lea! You *have* to take photos with me. It'll be so much more fun!"

"Okay," I said, thrilled. "Maybe we could sell prints to raise money for the animal sanctuary in Brazil where they're taking care of the baby sloth!"

Abby clapped her hands together. "Great idea!"

As Abby started making plans, my gaze drifted across the crowd. By the entrance, a woman in a

purple velvet dress caught my eye. As she turned her head, I recognized Hallie! I had told her about the COCA exhibit, but I'd never expected her to actually come. Yet here she was, leaning on Justus.

I grabbed Mom's hand and dragged her across the room. Hallie's face lit up when I told her Mom was Ama's daughter.

"It's so wonderful to meet you," she said, clasping Mom's hand.

"Thank you both so much for coming," Mom said to Hallie and Justus. "Are you a fan of photography?" she asked Hallie.

"I'm a fan of Lea," Hallie said, eyes sparkling. "When she told us about the exhibit, I thought, now there's something I'd like to see. And my son is a big fan of COCA."

"I helped raise funds for the restoration a few years ago," Justus said. "This building is a St. Louis landmark, and those should be preserved."

"I couldn't agree more," said my mother.

Suddenly, my brain was about to burst with an idea. "Mr. Dumond, what do you do?" I asked.

He looked surprised. "I'm a commercial real

estate developer," he replied.

"Really?" I said eagerly. "Do you ever fix up old buildings? Because my mom's trying to save this amazing house in Old North St. Louis and make it into a community center."

"Lea," Mom broke in. She seemed embarrassed, but my mind was moving too fast to stop.

"The building she's fixing up is Coventry House, where you and Ama went to school," I told Hallie. Then I turned to Justus. "But the funding fell through, so now it may get torn down."

"Lea, please," said Mom. "We don't need to discuss it."

"Actually, we *should* discuss it," said Hallie, turning to her son. "Lea's right. Coventry House is an important piece of this city's architectural history. It would be a terrible shame to lose it after all these years."

"I'd like to see the project," Justus said.

"Really?" Mom said. I could hear the surprise in her voice.

Justus nodded. "I've been looking to do a historical renovation. I just haven't found the right project.

This one sounds promising."

"You two discuss it," Hallie said, "while Lea shows me her photographs."

She leaned on me as we walked over to my pictures, but I was the one who was shaking. I really wanted her to like my work. First, I showed her the photo of Camila and Abby at the mural. She looked at it for a long moment, studying the faces.

"I remember this mural," she said wistfully. "I'm so glad it's being brought back to life. And your photo is extraordinary."

"Thank you," I said. Hallie turned, studying the two portraits of herself on the wall nearby. When she finally looked back at me, her eyes began to tear up.

"Looking at this makes me realize how lucky I've been," she said. "I had so many dreams for adventure as a girl, and fulfilled so many of them. I wish the same thing for you," she said, and as she smiled, I felt like I was glowing.

The rest of the evening went by in a blur. Mom and Dad both loved my photos. Dad even tried to call Zac in Brazil on video chat to show him the exhibit, but there was no answer. So we left a crazy

rushed message asking him to call us back, and I used Dad's phone to e-mail Zac my photos. Then it seemed like everyone in the room wanted to talk to me about the Hallie photographs—how I'd found the first picture and how I'd gotten the idea for the new portrait. I talked so much that my mouth got dry and Dad had to get me a cup of water.

"You should add 'detective' to your list of accomplishments," he said as he handed it to me.

Justus really liked my portrait of Hallie. He even said he wanted to buy it, but I told him I would make him a copy for free. That made him smile. Right after that, my mom whispered to me that it was "looking good" that Justus would fund the restoration of the Coventry House! I felt like I was floating on air.

Finally, people started to leave. As Justus went to get Hallie's coat, I sat next to her on a leather bench, across from the mosaic of the St. Louis skyline. "Thank you again for coming," I said. Hallie turned to me, the compass necklace swaying around her neck.

"I should thank *you*," she said. "You brought Amanda back into my life, along with so many good memories." I flushed, pleased.

 Picture Perfect

"You remind me so much of your grandmother as a girl, Lea," Hallie said. "Like Amanda, you have a truly adventurous spirit. I want to make sure you never lose that, no matter what life throws at you." With shaking hands, Hallie bent her head and slipped off her compass necklace. "I want you to have this," she said, extending it to me.

"Oh, no," I said, "I can't. It's too special—it's your last link with Ama—"

"That's *why* you should have it!" Hallie exclaimed, and pressed it into my hand. "It's for you to keep forever, so you can remember Ama and me. Your grandmother had total faith that both our lives would be great adventures," she said, "as long as we weren't afraid to go after what we wanted. Now, that spirit of adventure lives on in you."

Hallie hung the compass around my neck. I was almost crying, but at the same time, my heart felt like it was flying. As I hugged Hallie, feeling Ama's compass connecting us, I remembered the promise Hallie and Ama had made to each other, to follow their dreams. I was part of that now, too, and I knew it was one promise I would always keep.

A Return to Brazil

Chapter 14

The morning Camila was going to fly home, I helped her pack. We squashed her clothes and the St. Louis Cardinals foam finger inside her suitcase, and I sat on top so she could zip it shut. By the time we rolled the suitcase out of Zac's room and carried it downstairs, we had just enough time for a quick snack. My mom gave us glasses of milk and some leftover squares of gooey butter cake to eat on the porch.

Outside, the weather was perfect. Daffodils and crocuses were in bloom along the footpath leading from our porch to the Hickory Street sidewalk, and the air smelled like flowers and wet grass. "I will miss St. Louis," Camila said, as we sat on the front steps. "The buildings and the gardens . . ."

"Not to mention the gooey butter cake," I said,

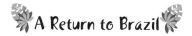

taking a bite. She laughed. "Especially the gooey butter cake!" she said. Then she looked serious. "Most of all, I will miss you, Lea."

"I'll miss you too!" I said. "And I want to say thank you," I added. "You and Abby helped me find Hallie."

Camila looked pleased. "It was a great adventure," she said. Suddenly, she jumped up. "I almost forgot!" She raced inside and came back a minute later with a small plastic tube. "I got you a gift," she said, handing it to me.

"Really?" I said, pleased. I took the blue cap off the end of the tube and held it up, and a rolled-up paper slipped out. Carefully, I uncurled it to reveal a colorful, antique-looking map of St. Louis. The writing was spidery and old-fashioned, but I could still read the markings for Lafayette Square, Old North St. Louis, Forest Park, and the Jewel Box. "This is so cool!" I exclaimed.

"It is from the History Museum," Camila said. "Now you have a map of St. Louis for your room. To remind you to keep exploring even when you are at home."

 **Lea and Camila**

Mom and I drove Camila to the airport and waited while she boarded the plane to Chicago. As she moved down the walkway out of sight, sadness crept up on me. I had no idea if I'd ever see Camila or Brazil again. *Someday*, I thought to myself, *I'm going to return to Brazil.* But when? It seemed impossible that I'd ever get a chance to go back there. Still, I thought about running on the golden beaches and trekking through dense rainforest with howler monkeys and sloths during the entire ride back to Lafayette Square.

Mom's cell phone rang as we were walking up to our house. She picked up.

"Hello, Mr. Dumond," she said, her voice catching with excitement. "You did? . . . Really? That's wonderful. I'll have my office call yours to set up a meeting on Monday." Mom hung up the phone and turned to me, her eyes shining.

"It's official. Justus Dumond is going to fund the Coventry House project!" she exclaimed, a grin bursting onto her face. "We don't have to worry about it being torn down!"

I yelped with excitement and hugged her. "You did it!"

"Actually, Lea, I think *you* did it," Mom said, giving me a squeeze. "Thank you for having the courage to mention the project to him. Now Coventry House will be part of both St. Louis's past *and* its future. You've helped to protect an important piece of the city's history."

Mom's words made me glow inside. As I hugged her again, I thought about all the people in the community who would get a chance to spend time at Coventry House now. I felt really proud that I'd done something to help make that possible.

While Mom called her partners to let them know the good news, I checked my e-mail. My heart did a happy skip when I saw a new message from Zac:

Your photos are awesome. Seriously, you are an amazing photographer! And I can't believe how you tracked down Hallie. You really proved that you're Ama's granddaughter!

Zac had attached a few photos of the baby

macaws, who now had a lot more feathers. As I read the rest of his e-mail, however, I could tell that the situation there wasn't great.

The poachers here have gotten more active. They tried cutting the wire fence around the sanctuary. And they even stole Wylie, our golden tamarin monkey with the broken arm. It's bad enough that they're hunting healthy animals, but stealing an injured monkey? That's truly evil.

As I read, anger rose inside me.

They've been growing bolder, but I've been growing bolder, too. I've researched their tracking patterns and how they keep and smuggle the animals they're taking. The next time they come after our animals, I'll be ready.

My stomach twisted around itself in anxiety. What Zac was doing sounded dangerous. I kept reading.

I know the risks and I'm prepared. Someone needs
to protect these animals. Don't worry about me,
Lea, I know what I'm doing—it's only the most
important work I've ever done.
Hugs, Z.

I stared at the computer screen for a long moment after I finished reading. I was worried about
Zac, but I knew he was right. It *was* up to all of us to
save and protect the things we cared about—just the
way I had saved Amanda the baby sloth, and Abby
had saved Dodger, and Mom was saving Coventry
House. In a way I wished I could be back in the
rainforest with Zac. It sounded dangerous and truly
scary, but I agreed with him: Saving wild animals
from evil poachers seemed like the most important
work anyone could do.

About the Author

Lisa Yee has written over a dozen books for young people. She loves to do research and was thrilled when Lea's stories took her to the Bahia coast of Brazil. There, she snorkeled among the coral reefs, sampled local foods, and learned about the traditions and customs of the region. Lisa also visited the Amazon rainforest, where she fished for piranhas, swam in the Amazon River, and even ate roasted insect larvae during a hike through the rainforest. However, the highlights of her travels were meeting a caiman, a boa constrictor, and a baby sloth—though not all at once!

You can learn more about Lisa at www.lisayee.com and see photos of her Brazilian adventures.

About the Author

Kellen Hertz was born in Canada and raised in California's Central Valley. She started her first novel at twelve, which was tragically left unfinished after the first chapter became lost in a sea of library books on the floor of her room. She overcame her sorrow by reading and writing a lot, and then went to Yale and UCLA and read and wrote some more. She's written plays and screenplays, directed a movie, and written or produced over 80 hours of prime-time and cable television. She loves flea markets, old maps, coffee, words and all the flavors they come in, and most of all, her family. She lives with her husband and son in Los Angeles.